A Woman's Guide to
BLACKJACK

A Woman's Guide to
BLACKJACK

———◆———

TURNING THE TABLES
WHEN THE CARDS ARE
STACKED AGAINST YOU

Angie Marshall

A LYLE STUART BOOK
Published by Carol Publishing Group

A Lyle Stuart Book
Published by Carol Publishing Group
Lyle Stuart is a registered trademark of Carol Communications, Inc.

Editorial, sales and distribution, and rights and permissions inquiries should be addressed to Carol Publishing Group, 120 Enterprise Avenue, Secaucus, N.J. 07094.

In Canada: Canadian Manda Group, One Atlantic Avenue, Suite 105, Toronto, Ontario M6K 3E7

Carol Publishing Group books may be purchased in bulk at special discounts for sales promotion, fund-raising, or educational purposes. Special editions can be created to specifications. For details, contact Special Sales Department, Carol Publishing Group, 120 Enterprise Avenue, Secaucus, N.J. 07094.

Manufactured in the United States of America
10   9   8   7   6   5   4   3   2   1

Library of Congress Cataloging-in-Publication Data

Marshall, Angie.
  A woman's guide to blackjack : turning the tables when the cards are stacked against you / Angie Marshall.
     p.   cm.
  "A Lyle Stuart book."
  Includes bibliographical references.
  ISBN 0–8184–0606–2 (pbk.)
  1. Blackjack (Game)   2. Women gamblers.   I. Title.
GV1295.B55M39   1999
795.4'23'082—dc21   98–48110
                                         CIP

Chandeliers

Just a Woman
*   playing their game*
They think I don't know how
*   oh, what a shame!*

Their chandeliers sparkle
*   motivating my play*
But I don't let the glitter
*   get in my way.*

Slowly, secretly,
*   one small piece at a time*
The chandeliers become mine
*   to have and to shine.*

—ANGIE

CONTENTS

TIDBITS

🔸 Gaming is now the nation's favorite pastime. More individuals gamble than the combined total of those attending movies, sports, music events, theme parks, and live entertainment.

• The number of individuals participating in gaming has doubled in the last five years.

• Las Vegas has more than one hundred thousand hotel rooms. Four of the five largest hotels in the world are located in Las Vegas.

• Las Vegas currently has 123 casinos, 1,700 blackjack tables, and employs five thousand blackjack dealers.

• Thirty states now allow casino gambling.

• More female gamblers (now totaling almost twenty-two million) are choosing blackjack as a destination game—one where they plan to spend a significant amount of their recreational time and money.

• Two years in a row, a female blackjack player won the Riviera National Finals Blackjack Championship.

A Woman's Guide to
BLACKJACK

1

Just a Woman

Just a Woman
  playing their game
They think I don't know how,
  oh, what a shame!

—ANGIE

In the world of casino gambling, women have a unique opportunity. At the blackjack tables, we are dismissed as barely functional—certainly not a threat. Yes, chauvinism is alive and well in the casinos—and I love it!

Gambling is the fastest growing industry in our society, and women are a large part of it. An estimated twenty-two million women now gamble each year. Most try their luck at blackjack, but few are aware of its opportunities.

Blackjack is the *only* casino game which can be beaten with skilled play, and casino personnel are deathly afraid of skilled players. Their job is to protect the casino bank, and good players are a threat to that bank. They will scrutinize every male blackjack player for any clue that he may have mastered the game, and believe me (or at least believe my husband, Steven), they won't hesitate to take action against any man who they believe poses a threat. All this activity and paranoia occurs while women go virtually unnoticed at the tables. We couldn't have created a better gambling environment even if we had designed it ourselves!

Just being women gives us a built-in edge. Lance Humble and Carl Cooper, in their book *The World's Greatest Blackjack Book*, have a section entitled "Be a Woman," which talks about the chauvinistic attitude of casino personnel and the total lack of respect women get as gamblers. They mention knowing men who disguise themselves as women just to take advantage of this attitude. In his book *Playing Blackjack As a Business*, the late Lawrence Revere observed that "most pit bosses believe that all female players are stupid." Normally we despise these beliefs, but in blackjack we should love it. Max Rubin, in his 1994 book *Comp City*, dedicates three pages to women, how the casino bosses view them, and how to take advantage of their attitude. Mr. Rubin was a casino boss with years of experience, and his conclusion that "bosses don't feel there's a reason to fear or suspect women" is to our benefit. So let's put that edge to work!

The edge is certainly real, and the strategies which allow me (and which will soon allow you) to take full advantage of the opportunities are very effective. They evolved as my awareness of the possibilities available to women became more apparent. The formula I use is actually a combination of necessities (required mechanics), refinements (which reduce the complex to the practical), and style (which allows me to play a winning strategy and act like a typical player). I now play with confidence and a self-reliance which eluded me up until a few years ago. I have fun, I win, and I have seldom been under close scrutiny by casino personnel. I have even watched in complete amazement as Steven was kicked out of a casino while I was left sitting at the table—completely ignored! However, this incident did instill in me the need for a healthy balance between skill and caution.

For you, learning will be much easier than it was for me, but please don't get the idea that you can start building a casino chandelier collection by simply reading this book. No deception...casino chandeliers are available, but acquiring one will take work, study, and practice. While thinking about this, keep in mind that casino operators don't believe you are capable. They are wrong. After all, I learned—and I'm "just a woman."

I hope you enjoy this book as much as I enjoyed writing it, and I hope you have as much fun at the tables as I do!

2

Explaining the Game

The recipe for perpetual ignorance is to be satisfied
with your opinions and content with your knowledge.

—ELBERT HUBBARD

Blackjack is played on a special table, or on a kitchen table, in every state and in most towns. You can wager your money on games run by large corporate casinos, local charity organizations, Indian reservations, or individuals in their homes. It is the most popular table game in existence, and it is growing so rapidly that it is hard to keep up with. It's wonderful. It may be the most exciting time in history to be a knowledgeable female blackjack player.

Learning anything requires a beginning. You can't expect to purchase a computer and simply start surfing the Internet. First, you would have to learn computer lingo and to find your way around the keyboard. Learning blackjack is no different.

If you were to ask a dealer to explain how to play, you might get this answer: "There's nothing to it. I'll give you two cards, and me two cards, and I'll even turn one of my cards up so you can see it. You can get more cards if you want, and if you get closer to 21 than I do without going over, you win. If you go over, or bust, the hand is over and I win. If you don't bust, then it's my turn, and if I bust then you win and the hand is over. If we tie, nobody wins. Aces count as one or eleven, and if you choose one, then it's a hard hand, and if you choose eleven, then it's soft. You can double-down if you want, but only on your first two cards, and you can split pairs if you like, but you've got to bet the same on the second one and then play them both just like it was your only one, unless your pair was Aces, then you will get just one card on those, and if you get a blackjack I'll pay you three for two, but not if you get it on the Aces you split. But if I get a blackjack then I get just your bet and no more, except you could have kept your bet if you had taken insurance, and, oh, I forgot, if you get another card like the one you split, you can split it again if you want, but you have to pay more and then you have to play it like a regular hand, unless the pair was Aces, then you can't split those again, at least not here, but sometimes they will let you downtown. I have to hit on 16 and stand on 17, except if it's a soft 17, then I have to hit it again. You have to buy-in, but see, there's nothin' to it, so you ready to play or what?"

You may have gotten this the first time, but if you are like me you may want to go over it again—a little slower. Some of the casinos have rookie tables where dealers give instructions on the game. At these tables you will play blackjack with tokens, ask as many questions as you want, and play with dealers who are very patient and helpful. Sometimes the instructors will even offer good advice. "Hazel" is one of these instructors. Let's listen in as she teaches "Angel" to play.

Hazel is an elderly lady and obviously chosen because of her public relations abilities. She greets this lady as she sits down at her table. "Good afternoon, and welcome to the table of the world's greatest blackjack instructor. As you can see, modesty is not one of my vices. Where you from?"

"Los Angeles, and I don't know anything about this game."

"Well Miss L.A.—I'll just call you Angel—you came to the right place. You remind me a lot of my daughter. She's a little older, but you look a lot like her. Anyway, my name is Hazel, and anytime you have a question, just stop me and ask away. Get over any feelings about asking dumb questions right now, because there is no such thing. I've been dealing blackjack for over twenty years and I've seen and heard it all, so don't be bashful."

"Okay, but I'll probably have lots of dumb questions."

"I just told you there is no such thing. Let's start with me showing you around the table. I am standing immediately behind the chip tray. I have fifty-cent pieces here which I need to pay off blackjacks, that's a 21 on your first two cards. If you get a blackjack, then you are paid three-to-two for your bet. So if you bet five dollars, you would be paid seven dollars and fifty cents. That's why I need fifty-cent pieces.

"Dollar chips are next to them. Here they are silver, but some casinos use white chips for dollars. Next to those I have red chips, which are worth five dollars each. We call them nickels. The green chips are worth twenty-five dollars; we call them quarters. The black chips are worth one hundred dollars each, called bucks in casino lingo. The color of chips are pretty much standard among casinos.

"Here on my left is a shoe that we will deal out of if we use more than two decks. If you sit at a table that uses just one or two decks, then the cards will be dealt from the hand.

"This little sign that says blackjack instruction will normally give the table minimum and maximum bets. Look at that table behind you. The sign says five-dollar minimum and five-hundred-dollar maximum. It just means you have to bet at least five dollars on each hand and no more than five hundred dollars per hand.

"Here on my right is a currency slot. When you give the dealer cash he will give you an equal value in chips and then pull out this paddle, lay your money right here, and then slide the paddle back in. Your money disappears forever, only to be seen by cross-eyed little accountants in the back room. Next to it is the discard tray where all the cards are placed after they have been played."

"I have a question."

"Angel, I thought I told you not to interrupt me! Just joking. Where did I lose you?"

"You didn't lose me, but I was wondering. Why do they call five-dollar chips nickels and twenty-five-dollar chips quarters?"

"To reduce the significance of money. Casinos don't want you to worry about money, so calling five dollars a nickel kinda helps that, I guess. When I first started to work we called the dollar chips pennies and the dollar tables penny tables. There aren't many dollar tables around any more; most have gone to two-dollar minimums, and there aren't even too many of those. They are actually called two-dollar tables; calling them two-penny tables sounds a little awkward. You ready to go on?"

"Yeah, thanks."

"Okay, the house rules, which the dealer has to follow, are normally written right here in front of the chip tray. As you can see, the dealer has to hit sixteen and stand on seventeen. Just below that, toward you, is an insurance band. If the dealer has an Ace showing, you can insure your hand by placing an amount equal to one-half your bet in this band. Insurance pays two to one, so if you take it and the dealer has a blackjack then he will pay you twice your insurance bet. You would lose your original bet to the dealer's blackjack—unless you also had a blackjack—but even if you lose your original bet, you still break even because of the insurance payoff. Sounds better than it is—taking insurance is generally not a good idea.

"Right in front of you is a betting circle where you must place your bet. In some casinos it will be a square or a symbol, but whatever it is, you must place your bet on it. If you place it beside the circle, like this, then the dealer will ask you what your intentions are, or will simply deal past you and leave you out of that hand. Don't touch your bet if the dealing has started, because it may look like you are trying to cheat by adding more chips when you have a good hand, or removing a few if you have a bad hand. Take my word for it, you don't want the misery the bosses can give you if they think you are cheating."

"I have another question. Back to insurance—why did you say it's not a good idea to take it? What if I have a good hand, say a twenty or a blackjack. Wouldn't it be good to insure them?"

"That's a good question. You're pretty smart for a lady who chooses to live on a perpetual earthquake. Angel, I hope I can tease you without offending you because when I like somebody that's what I do. Anyway, don't let the term insurance fool you. They would probably fire me if they knew I was telling you this, but it really doesn't insure a damn thing. It's just a side bet, and doesn't have anything to do with your hand. They even make you insure at half your original bet to make you think it really is insurance. About thirty-one percent of the cards in a deck are tens—that includes face cards, which count as tens. If you took insurance for a hundred hands you would expect the dealers to have a ten under their Ace only thirty-one percent of the time. Even with a two-to-one payoff, you still lose in the long run, so don't take it. Now you mind ol' Hazel, 'cause she knows what she's talking about.

"All right, in a minute we'll play a few hands, and I'll teach you about playing the game. I'll just use one deck, and I'll give you some tokens to bet with. But first I need to tell you about buying in—buying the chips to get into the game. To do that just lay your cash here, beside your betting circle. Don't put it in your circle or you might end up playing it. You can actually bet currency if you want to, but chips are much easier to handle. Anyway, when you win you will be paid in chips, so you might as well buy in to begin with. The dealer will take your money and spread it out in the middle of the table to count it and let pictures be taken of it. Look up above you. Those black domes on the ceiling contain video cameras that have lenses pointed at each table. The videos are used to settle disputes, and verify buy-in amounts, card totals, and payoffs. We call it the eye-in-the-sky. After the dealer counts the money, he'll give you an equal amount in chips. Dealers don't give change, so the money you put on the table will be changed for chips.

"We're almost ready to deal. I'll shuffle first and then we'll play a few hands. That green plastic card I just gave you is the cut card. Place it in the deck wherever you want and I'll cut the deck right there. You have to cut at least eight cards below the top or above the bottom of the deck. It's policy in this casino. Good. Now I'll move the cards in front of your cut to the back of the deck. Then I burn the top card by placing it here in the discard tray.

"Remember, in this game your goal is to get closer to 21 than I do. If you exceed 21, you bust and lose. This part's so basic I sometimes forget that some people don't know it: each card from 2 through 10 is equal to it's face value, all the face cards—the Jacks, Queens and Kings—count 10 each, and Aces are 1 or 11. If you have a 2 and an 8, you have 10. Then, if you draw a Queen you would have 20. Don't worry, we'll practice.

"Okay, you've got to bet before I start to deal. Play like you just bought in, and here's fifty dollars in funny-money chips. You're betting one chip. Good for you, now we're moving.

"I deal by starting with the player on my left and give each player one card to begin with. I deal to myself last, face down. I'll then do it again, only this time I'll turn my second card up. This time I'm dealing both cards to the players face down but some casinos deal face up, so in a minute I'll show you what that's like.

"Okay, you can see that I have a 7 for my up-card, and you don't know what my other card is; we call that the hole card. What have you got? An 8 and a 5. Ugh. You'll want to take a hit on 13 against my 7, so you do that by scratching the cards on the table like you're trying to move a speck on the felt. That's right, now I'll give you your hit card face up. A 7! Not bad, now you have a 20, so you're going to want to stand. You do that by sliding the edge of your cards under your bet, like this. When you have done that it tells me that you are satisfied. Then I'll turn my hole card up and finish my hand. Okay, I had a 10 in the hole, so your 20 beats my 17. I will now pay you and gather the used cards and place them in the discard tray. If you had busted, you would turn your cards face up on the table and I would take your cards and your bet before I went on to the next player. If we had tied—we call it pushing— you would have kept your bet.

"Before I forget, let me show you what a face-up game looks like. In that game, all the cards are face up except for my hole card. Your 8 and 5 would be face up, like this. When you need a hit you just scratch your fingers on the felt—that's the way—and after you get your hit and decide that you don't want more cards just move your hand over the top of your cards, palm down, like you're trying to see if any heat is coming off of them. If there is, you be sure and tell me, 'cause there would be something bad wrong!"

"I have another question: Why don't I just tell you when I want a hit or when I want to stand, instead of scratching and waving?"

It's because of the noise in these casinos. If you told me you wanted a hit I might not hear you, or I might misunderstand and go on to the next player. You would then be upset, and when the boss came over to settle the dispute, it would be your word against mine and he would have to decide what to do. When hand signals are used there is less confusion, and if a serious dispute does occur, it can easily be settled by reviewing the tape from the eye-in-the-sky. It doesn't happen very often, but sometimes at high-stakes games disputes can be serious. Hand signals are required at most casinos as a matter of policy."

"Thanks. Before you go on, can you tell me why some casinos deal face-up games?"

"Angel, you're full of good questions. Dealing face up is done primarily to protect the cards. In those games you are not allowed to touch the cards. They last longer since they aren't being handled so much. It also keeps cheaters from marking the cards with little bends or scratches. Some casinos are paranoid about that. Also, in face-up or face-down games you are not allowed to touch another player's cards. Dealers have to play by set rules, so seeing your cards doesn't give the casino an advantage. You ready to go on? Good. I'll tell you a little about Aces. By the way, your questions are good, so keep it up. Okay, Aces count as 1 or 11—your choice. They will probably cause you a lot of grief at first, but it will get easier as you get some experience. If you get an Ace or have more than one Ace in your hand and get confused about the total, just ask the dealer what you have. The important thing is not to let dealers fluster you, and don't be embarrassed to ask one for help.

"Now I'll tell you about two playing options: doubling-down and splitting pairs. Let me pick out the cards for our hands to show you what you can do with them. Okay, here is a 6 and a 4 for you, and a 4 for my up-card. We don't know what my hole card is, but you have a total of 10, a pretty good hand against my 4. You now have the option of doubling-down if you want to. You can actually double on any first two cards, but you're not going to want to unless it's to your advantage. To double-down, simply place an equal amount of chips beside your original bet and turn your two cards face up. The dealer will give you one card face down, like this. Remember, when you double-down you only get one more card, so be sure that is what you want to do. Okay, let's see how you did. My hole card is a 10, so I now have 14. I have to take a hit, so...another 10. I busted. What have you got? An 8. See, you won your double-down hand and twice the money you would have if you had chosen to hit instead of doubling.

"Are you still with me? Good, now let me set you up with a pair— two cards of the same value—and I'll tell you about splitting. Here's two 9s for your hand. Let's give me an 8 for an up-card. In this situation, you can split your 9s by turning them up on the table in front of your bet and placing another bet equal to your first beside your original bet. That's the way. Now the dealer will separate the two cards and give you a hit, face up, on your first 9. Okay, you drew a 10 for your first hit. You now have 19 for that hand and probably want to stand. Right? Good.

"Now you have to tell me you want to stand by using hand signals. No, no, you look like you're swatting flies. Do it palm down, like you're trying to feel heat. That's right, you got it now.

"Okay, on to the next 9...a 2 for your hit card. Now you have another decision to make. We allow doubling after splits, so you can double-down on your 11 if you want. That's a pretty good double-down hand against my 8. You want to try it? Okay, I'm only going to give you one card, and it will be face down, just like all the other double-down hands. Now I go to my hand. I have a 7 in the hole, so I have to hit. I got a 3, so that gives me an 18 and I have to stand. You won your first split with a 19, and you have a 10 under your second hand, for a 21. You win all the way across. You're pretty lucky when you're playing with funny money.

"There is another thing you need to know about splitting pairs: if the pair you drew were Aces you could split them, but you only get one card to each Ace. If you draw another Ace, then you can't resplit. You just have to live with two Aces for one of your hands. It wouldn't be a very good hand, but you would be stuck with it. And if you drew a 10 to your Ace it would give you 21, but not a blackjack, because blackjacks can only happen on the first two cards dealt during a hand."

"I've got another question. What do you mean when you say resplit?"

"Thanks, Angel, I guess I forgot to explain that. First, though, the cocktail waitress is coming. They serve you free drinks even when you're playing with fake money. You want one? Okay, order your drink, then I'll tell you about resplitting.

"Okay, If you had drawn another 9 awhile ago on one of the 9s you had already split, then you could have split again. Most places will let you split up to four times. Again, whether or not you would want to depends on your cards and the dealer's up-card. Many times this will provide a good opportunity for the player. Thanks again for reminding me. This can be confusing enough without me leaving out important stuff.

"Here comes your drink. If you have any change in your purse you should tip the waitress. They don't make much, and they have to walk around here all day with hardly any clothes on. A lot of the men tip them pretty good, but we should also tip a little. Listen, Angel, don't drink too much when you're playing blackjack. I've seen lots of people start acting rich when they drink and they generally end up losing their shirt. The men in here would like that, but I doubt that you'd be too happy about it. Enough of my motherly advice, at least for a minute. Let's move on. We'll play for a while, and more questions may pop up as we go along."

"I've got one already: Since you mentioned tipping the waitress, what about tipping the dealers?"

"Well, that's up to you, but it is customary. A lot of the dealers depend on tips to make their car payments, so it's kind of part of their salary. It used to be that the nicer we were to the players, the more tips we'd make. Some dealers made more on tips than they did in their salary, but now all the tips go in a pot and are split with all the rest of the dealers. That way if one dealer gets lucky dealing to a high roller, then the other dealers share in the good fortune. It's not really fair, I don't think, because some of the dealers are real jerks and would hardly get any tips, but I have to share with them anyway. Oh, well, I guess I could retire if it started grating on me too much. Or I could move to a casino where the dealers get to keep their own tips, but there aren't many of them. Anyway, tipping is customary.

"Some dealers prefer you just give them a tip, but most dealers prefer that you place a bet for them. To do that you place the tip here, at the top of the betting circle above your bet. Place the tipping bet there before the deal starts, and if you win the hand, then the dealer will pay off both bets. If you lose, then both bets are lost to the casino. Most dealers like the betting tip better because it lets them play the game while they are working. I'm full of free advice today, but you shouldn't tip too much, unless, of course, you are playing at my table! I've seen players walk away from a table a loser just because they tipped too much.

"Okay, back to practice. I'll deal a few hands so you can get a feel for the game before you move on to the real tables. Most players raise their bets now and then when they think they're going to win, so you might try that while you're playing with tokens. Good. Now, if you have any questions about your hand or the game, remember to ask. What have you got this time? A 16, and I have a 10 showing. Rotten! You now have the worst hand you can draw at this game. Some casinos have a 'surrender rule,' but we don't offer it here. I know they offer it down the street at Harrah's. If you're playing at a casino where they offer it and you have a really lousy hand, just tell them you surrender and give the dealer your cards. He will then take one-half of your bet. Sure beats losing all of it. But since we don't offer it, do you want to hit or stand? A hit. Okay, your card is an 8—you bust. Don't expect to win them all.

"Once more, place your bet and we'll start again. Wow! You must really think you're going to win the next hand, betting ten chips. Well, good luck. If I was dealing to you over there at the regular tables, I would have to announce 'checks play' so the pit boss would know that a player is significantly raising her bet. We don't have a boss here, so I'll just wish you good luck. I've got a 10 showing. What have you got? An 18 I dunno, pretty weak, but let's see what happens. You want to stand, I see. I've got another 10 in the hole, so you lose. That was a pretty high bet when you had been betting only one or two at a time. What do you think you are, psychic or something?"

"Another question. Why do you say 'checks play?' What does it mean, and why does the pit boss care?"

"I'm not sure where it originated, but it's been used since I've been dealing. One of the boss's jobs is to watch for card-counters, and one of the things he watches for is how wide a bet spread a player has. If a player all of a sudden bets big, then I have to announce it by saying 'checks play.' The pit boss will then make a note to watch that player more closely.

"See the guy walking around behind the tables over there? The one with the red tie who looks like he has a perpetual toothache? That's Andy. He's been a boss here for about a year and thinks he can smell card-counters, but he really can't. Good card-counters don't act like they know much and hardly ever get caught. I guess he can catch a bad one now and then, but they have to have a neon sign around their neck saying 'I count' before he would know for sure. I have dealt to some good counters, and I don't care if they win. They put in some work to get good, and I consider this a game of skill. If they have the skill and can win—well, more power to them. There are plenty of losers to more than make up for whatever they win. Anyway, that's just my idea, but it's certainly not shared by Andy."

"Is card-counting illegal?"

"Oh, no. There's nothing illegal about it. It's not cheating, but in Nevada the casinos have been able to maintain their status as privileged establishments. It just means that it is a privilege to play in the casinos, and they can deny that privilege anytime they think you have an advantage over them.

"Listen, Angel, I kind of like you, so I'm going to give you some more good advice. You've already shown that you're smart by learning the only casino game that can be beaten with skilled play. Why don't you learn to play it right? I've shown you *how* to do a lot of things, but you need to know *when* to do them. You need to know when to stand, or hit, and when you should double or split. You need to know when to bet big and when to bet the minimum.

"Most of the bosses and dealers, including women dealers, don't think women are smart enough to play this game right. Now I don't think that way, but they do. Some think you ought to be at home folding sheets, or that you'd be better at wrinkling them. Now don't get mad, it's just what they think, but their attitude can work to your benefit. Angel, my grandmother used to tell me, 'It's not what people *think* you know that counts, it's *what* you know.'

"There is a dandy blackjack book out that's written specifically for women. Get it and learn how to play this game good enough to win. Yours truly, ol' Hazel, is mentioned in the book, so it must be good, right? I thought you would agree. You leaving already? Oh, you're going to get the book! Well, go on, and I'll talk to you later!"

Chapter Overview

Hazel did a good job of explaining the table layout, how to buy in and place bets, information about player options, tipping, casino policy, and table etiquette, but I would like you to turn to chapter 13, "Casino Lingo," at the back of the book and read the definitions before you go on. You won't remember everything there, but at least you will know what it contains so you can refer to it when you need to.

Let's follow Hazel's advice and learn how to play the game right. The following chapter will be the beginning of your road to blackjack success.

3

The Basics

The great dividing line between success and failure
can be expressed in five words. "I did not have time."

—FRANKLIN FIELD

I have observed players all over the United States and have come to the
conclusion that most people let chance, hope, and intuition guide their
actions. Either they don't know, don't believe, or don't care that there is
a right way to play *every single hand*. I have watched players repeatedly
make mistakes that would make even the grouchiest pit boss smile.
Don't get me wrong, I know there have to be losers, because if not there
wouldn't be casinos, but you and I don't have to be among those ranks.
Let someone else contribute to the happiness of pit bosses.

This chapter is serious, and it is an absolute must that you learn, and
I mean really *learn*, everything in it if you expect to cut the casino
advantage down to something manageable and provide yourself with
the foundation necessary to learn winning methods. Please study it and
learn it, whether it takes two days, or two months. Realistically, I think it
will only take you about two weeks. Once you have done this, you will
be ahead of 90 percent of all other players and will be on your way.

The first thing I want you to consider is finding a partner to study and
learn with. This person might be a girlfriend, boyfriend, relative, or your

husband. I was lucky and had a built-in partner (slave driver) who was willing to help me. You can certainly do it without one, but you will find that the small support group has more fun during this period and will sometimes get you to continue when you might find it easier to do something else. Your partner should be interested in blackjack and willing to go with you to Las Vegas. Give this some serious thought, because it will not only help you learn, it will provide many opportunities later.

The second thing I would like you to do is start thinking about establishing a gambling fund. This is important because I want you to go to Las Vegas in a few weeks! If you already have enough set aside, don't spend it, and if you don't have enough, then start saving right now! How much is enough? That depends on where you live. When I said Las Vegas, I meant *Las Vegas,* not Atlantic City, Biloxi, or Reno. Las Vegas offers the most diverse gambling conditions anywhere, and I want you to experience the good and the bad. Estimate your airfare or gas expenses, lodging and meals for two nights and three days, and car rental or taxi fare (if you fly), but, most important, pocket $300 for blackjack.

I am going to mention now, and again throughout the book, the critical importance of your gambling fund. I keep mine in a separate savings account, but wherever you choose to store yours, be sure that it contains *only* gambling money. No rent, food, or car payment money should be mixed with it. Odds are that you will be very good at blackjack in a few months, but even then, *never gamble with money you can't afford to lose!*

The third thing you need to do is schedule practice time. If you have found a partner, practice time must be mutually agreed upon. If you choose not to have a partner, then designate at least one hour per day of quiet time and protect it. Studying is not hard, but it is necessary to be able to do it without any interruptions.

The casinos don't buy more chandeliers, build more fountains, and add new one-thousand-room expansions because they are losing money. Blackjack is one of their "chandelier games," with estimates of casino advantage ranging from 2 to 5 percent, and greater, depending on the casino's rules—and how bad the players are! Learning to play good, basic-strategy blackjack cuts the casino advantage to an average of 0.5 percent—that's right—one-half of one percent! If you play basic strategy at a casino with *good rules* (one-deck game where you can double on any first two cards and double after splitting a pair), you can actually cut its advantage to 0.1 percent!

The following chart shows what strategy play can do for the player. I am including comparisons of typical "Jane" players to good basic-system players, and to count-systems players. For the casino advantage over the typical player I have used 3.5 percent. (Steven thinks the casino advantage is closer to 5 percent, so my estimates may be conservative.)

Under knowledge level, the chart shows what "expectation" a player would have. I have used an average bet of $10 for the typical and basic-system players (you are at a $5 table, where the average bet is generally about twice this minimum) and an average bet of $12.50 for the count-system player (my average bet under the count system is about 2.5 times the minimum). All three use an average of six hours of blackjack play per day, sixty hands per hour, based on a three-day trip. Take just a second to look at the definition of *action* in chapter 13, "Casino Lingo," in the back of the book. In this example, the action per hour is $10 (average bet) × 60 (hands or bets per hour) = $600 for typical and basic players. It is $750 for the count-system player. Pick your level of expertise, then go down the column under it and look at your loss or win expectation for each hour, day, and three-day trip.

Expectation at Various Levels of Expertise
($5 Table)

	Typical "Jane" Player	Basic-System Player	Count-System Player
Casino Advantage	3.5%	0.5%	
Player Advantage			1.5%
Average Bet	$10.00	$10.00	$12.50
Action/Hour	$600.00	$600.00	$750.00
Loss/Hour	$21.00	$3.00	
Win/Hour			$11.25
Loss/Day (6 Hrs.)	$126.00	$18.00	
Win/Day (6 Hrs.)			$67.50
Three-Day Loss	$378.00	$54.00	
Three-Day Win			$202.50

Learning the basic system reduces your average trip loss from $378 to $54. This *is* significant! It doesn't make you a winner, but you almost break even.

Since I have mentioned rules, I guess it is time to explain what this means. The largest single advantage a casino has over the player in blackjack hides in the "first to break" rule. This is really what makes blackjack a chandelier game for the casino, and simply means that if you bust, you lose, even if the dealer proceeds to bust during that same hand. However, other rules can go either way, with some contributing to *your* chandelier collection.

Casino Rules

Common Rules Favoring the Player

Double-down on any first two cards

Double after splitting (meaning you can double on a hand after you have split a pair)

Resplit pairs (meaning you can split again if you draw another card of the same value as the pair you originally split, generally allowed up to four times, not including aces)

Dealer stands on a soft 17

Uncommon Rules Favoring the Player

Double on any number of cards

Resplit Aces

Surrender

Special bonuses (two-for-one for three 7s, automatic win with a six-card no-bust, and others)

Rules Favoring the Casino

Doubling-down restricted to 10 or 11 only, or 9, 10, or 11 only

Dealer hits a soft 17

No resplitting of pairs

No doubling on soft totals (those that include Aces)

No surrender offered

No insurance offered (a good option for the card-counter)

The number of decks used in play is also very important. The more decks used, the higher the casino's advantage. The actual effect the rules and number of decks have on the player's advantage or disadvantage at any individual casino can be calculated during your trip, but it is so much easier to just look it up in one of the blackjack newsletters. We use, and highly recommend, Stanford Wong's *Current Blackjack News*. This particular newsletter gives the house advantage, with the player using basic strategy, for every casino in Nevada, Atlantic City, and states where blackjack is legal. Mr. Wong has reporters who keep him, and thus the newsletter, up to date. He reports on the number of tables being used at each casino, number of decks per table, and calculates the casino advantage. He also comments on the casino's rules and playing conditions. It saves a tremendous amount of time checking out each casino and evaluating its rules. If I ever meet Mr. Wong, I intend to give him a big kiss (I hope he's good-looking), for the amount of work he has saved us!

Hands With Aces

Now that you know about the rules, let's spend a few minutes talking about Aces. These are the nemesis of most beginning blackjack players, and rightfully so, because Aces just can't seem to make up their mind what they want to be. They can be valued as an 11 one minute and a 1 the next. Steven says they must be female (but don't worry, I'll get even with him for that one). All is not lost, however, because there is an easy way, or at least an easier way, to deal with them. As you start to learn the Basic Chart you will notice that it doesn't deal with expressions such as soft 16, or soft this or that. You will simply deal with Aces as Aces. For example, an Ace-5 is just that, an A,5, not a soft 16. If you draw more than one Ace, then automatically value any after the first as 1. So if you draw an A,5,A it becomes an A,6; an A,A,A,7 becomes an A,9. The Basic Chart will tell you what to do with the A,5 or the A,9, so start learning to deal with them in that way. If the Basic Chart tells you to hit on an A,6 and you then draw a 10 (you now have an A,6,10), the Ace automatically reverts to a value of 1. In that example, the Basic Chart doesn't have an A,16 listed; therefore, automatically deal with the Ace as a 1 for a hard 17 $(1+6+10=17)$. So, you either deal with Aces as Aces, or as 1. Still sound confusing? Have faith; it came to me fairly easily, so I know it will come to you. The Aces Practice Chart will help you. Ten-value cards are indicated with an X.

Aces Practice Chart

You Are Dealt	You Have	You Are Dealt	You Have
A,8	A,8	A,3	A,3
6,5,A	12	A,4,A	A,5
A,2,3	A,5	A,7	A,7
4,A,5	A,9	A,6,X	17
3,6,A	A,9	A,5,4	A,9
6,A,9	16	5,A,3	A,8
2,A,5	A,7	A,4,A,5	21
A,4,4	A,8	A,A	Pair
A,5,A	A,6	4,9,A	14
2,A,X	13	A,9	A,9
3,A,8	12	A,5,A	A,6
3,X,A	14	7,7,A	15
6,A,2	A,8	A,X	21
4,A,7,3	15	A,3,A,X	15
A,3,X,3,A	18	A,6,4	21

Basic Strategy

Basic strategy seems totally misnamed to me. It is so robust and powerful that simply calling it basic is like calling Elizabeth Taylor's biggest diamond just another rock. But it was named years ago, and since you may be wading through other reference books I won't confuse you by changing its name to something more appropriate.

To play winning blackjack, you first have to level the playing field between you and the casino, and the basic strategy does just that. The basics will teach you the proper way to play *every* single hand when you only know your two cards and what the dealer has for an up-card. Properly playing every hand will almost make you break even with the casino.

Some new blackjack players have a hard time believing in the accuracy of the basic strategy. Well, you have to! Computers have played billions of hands of blackjack (more than you and I could play in a hundred lifetimes). The results have shown that you will make more money in the long run by doubling-down on certain hands, that you will lose less money by hitting other hands, and so forth. You have to accept basic strategy as a given.

All right, it's time for you to look at the Basic Chart (page 35). The dealer's up-card is shown across the top of the chart and your hand is listed along the left-hand margin. The left-hand side of the chart is broken into five sections, based on similarities in players' hands and the strength of the dealer's up-card. The uppermost section (of the left-hand side) deals with your hands that total 8 through 11. The next section deals with hands that total 12 through 16; the next is A,2 through A,5; the next is A,6 through A,9; and the bottom deals with pairs. The dealer's up-card is also broken into sections, based on the strength of his cards. This method of breaking the chart into similarities results in the Basic Chart's "blocking." Memorizing the chart in block form will assist you in learning the individual hands later. A *D* means double-down, *S* means stand, *H* means hit, and the *Sp* means split. Ten-value cards are shown as *X*.

You may have noticed that no player totals less than 8 are listed. If you have 7 or less, you always hit. There are also no hard totals listed above 16. Please refer to chapter 13, "Casino Lingo," for an explanation of hard hands. If you have a hard total of 17 or more, you automatically stand. There is not a 4,4 or a 5,5 listed in the pairs (bottom) section because you *always* treat the 4,4 hand as 8 and the 5,5 hand as 10.

The chart is accurate for one-, two-, and four-deck games, but you will need to make seven changes to it if you have to play at tables with five or more decks. These changes are listed below the Basic Chart. For now, learn the chart as shown, and review the changes if you play at six- or eight-deck games. This will prepare you to play anywhere.

There is a tear-out copy of the chart in the back of the book. Remove it, make copies of it, and put one in your purse, car, bathroom, and everywhere else you spend time. Study it until you *know* it.

When I was learning the chart, I made the mistake of learning it "in order." I knew the chart, but I would have to visualize it before I could give the answer to any individual hand. To compensate, I made flash cards placing my hand and the dealer's up-card on the front and the proper action on the back. Then I would shuffle the flash cards and test myself until I knew each action without thinking. Try this and see if it helps you remember each action individually.

Cutting Losses

Most of the Basic Chart will make sense to you, but there are some oddball combinations. For example, why would you want to split on 8,8 (and double your bet) against a dealer's 10, or why would anyone in her right mind stand on a 7,7 against a dealer's 10? These are very legitimate questions. In any game, whether it be chess, bridge, basketball, or blackjack, there will be times when you are in a defensive mode. In this position, you are trying to cut your losses. The Basic Chart tells you to split a 8,8 against a 10, not because you will win if you do it, but because you will lose less than if you stood or hit. The same logic goes with standing on a 7,7 against a 10. You will lose less than if you split or hit.

The first section of the chart contains the hard double-down possibilities (your hands 8 through 11). Notice that with an 8 for your hand total, you will double only if the dealer has a 6 showing. However, if you have an 11, you will double against any dealer up card.

The second section contains the stiff hands (12 through 16), when the next card could cause you to bust. You will never double-down on these hands, and will stand anytime the dealer is likely to bust. Likewise, you will hit anytime the dealer is likely to complete a hand without busting. These are lousy hands to draw, but playing them correctly will reduce your losses.

The next two sections contain hands with Aces. The A,2 through A,5 section shows that you will double-down anytime the dealer has a 4, 5, or 6 for an up-card. Otherwise you hit. The A,6 through A,9 section is more of a mixture. While the logic that the chart shows may not be obvious for playing your Ace hands, follow it faithfully. (No female intuition allowed—that's what's "expected.")

The last section contains pairs, and the chart shows when you should split, hit, or stand. Always remember that the dealer does not have the option of splitting pairs (or doubling-down, or standing on a stiff hand), so take advantage of your options. The mathematics and statistics of the basic-play strategies have been calculated and proven in actual play. *Trust the chart.*

Basic Chart (One Through Four Decks)

Your Hand	Dealer's Up-card 2	3	4	5	6	7	8	9	X	A
8	H	H	H	H	D	H	H	H	H	H
9	D	D	D	D	D	H	H	H	H	H
10	D	D	D	D	D	D	D	D	H	H
11	D	D	D	D	D	D	D	D	D	D
12	H	H	S	S	S	H	H	H	H	H
13	S	S	S	S	S	H	H	H	H	H
14	S	S	S	S	S	H	H	H	H	H
15	S	S	S	S	S	H	H	H	H	H
16	S	S	S	S	S	H	H	H	H	H
A,2	H	H	D	D	D	H	H	H	H	H
A,3	H	H	D	D	D	H	H	H	H	H
A,4	H	H	D	D	D	H	H	H	H	H
A,5	H	H	D	D	D	H	H	H	H	H
A,6	D	D	D	D	D	H	H	H	H	H
A,7	S	D	D	D	D	S	S	H	H	H
A,8	S	S	S	S	D	S	S	S	S	S
A,9	S	S	S	S	S	S	S	S	S	S
A,A	Sp	Sp	Sp	Sp	Sp	Sp	Sp	Sp	Sp	Sp
2,2	H	Sp	Sp	Sp	Sp	Sp	H	H	H	H
3,3	H	H	Sp	Sp	Sp	Sp	H	H	H	H
6,6	Sp	Sp	Sp	Sp	Sp	H	H	H	H	H
7,7	Sp	Sp	Sp	Sp	Sp	Sp	H	H	S	H
8,8	Sp	Sp	Sp	Sp	Sp	Sp	Sp	Sp	Sp	Sp
9,9	Sp	Sp	Sp	Sp	Sp	S	Sp	Sp	S	S
X,X	S	S	S	S	S	S	S	S	S	S

Changes to the Basic Chart for Five Or More Decks

Hit an 8 against a 6
Hit a 9 against a 2
Hit an 11 against an Ace
Hit an A,2 against a 4
Hit an A,6 against a 2
Stand on an A,8 against a 6
Hit a 6,6 against a 2

Well, have you learned it? If so, you are now ahead of 90 percent of all other players. To be sure you really know it, try the Practice Chart listed on pages 28 and 29. This is a real test. This chart includes every possible hand that can be dealt to you, printed in random order, and requires you to total your first two cards. The first two numbers listed comprise your hand, and the one next to it is the dealer's up-card. Put the Basic Chart down next to you and try it. If you are not sure about the answer, look it up. Don't guess, and don't make mistakes! Vince Lombardi once said, "Practice does not make perfect; perfect practice makes perfect."

Good luck, and come back to me after you are able to complete the Practice Chart with confidence and without looking at your crib sheet. It might be easier to use the tear-out Practice Chart in the back of the book than the one in this chapter.

Basic Surrender

Surrender is an option offered only in a few Las Vegas casinos, but in other locations it is offered more regularly, so in the appropriate situation you need to know what to do. You lose half of your bet when you give up, so surrender only when you have a 15 against a dealer's 10, or when you have a 16 against a dealer's 9, 10, or Ace. When you have any of these hands, before you take any hits, just give the dealer your cards and say, "I surrender."

You are almost there. Just one more thing. In actual play you will often be required to make several consecutive decisions during the course of one hand. For example, you may be dealt a 5,2 for your first two cards. The dealer has a 10 up, you ask for a hit, and the dealer gives you an Ace. You now have an A,7 (bad) against a dealer's 10. The Basic Chart tells you to hit, so you do, and draw a 4. You now have a 12 (worse) against a 10, so you hit again and receive an 8. Now you have 20 (good) and can stand.

Situations like this are common in actual play, so break out a deck of cards and let's try it. Be sure there are no jokers in the deck, shuffle it and deal one card up for the dealer (that's all the dealer gets in this exercise) and two cards *up* to you. Dealing your cards face up means that you don't have to handle them as often. Complete your hand by hitting, splitting, doubling-down, or standing *exactly* as the Basic Chart indicates. On your double-down hands, just give yourself one more card down and pretend you doubled your bet. After you have completed your hand, gather the cards on the table and start a discard pile to your upper *left* (don't ask why right now, just do it). After you have practiced like this through about ten decks, start giving your ghost dealer two cards (one down) and then complete the dealer's hands to see if you won or lost. You can also start using chips (we use poker chips available at any discount store), and bet as if really playing. Practice like this until you feel comfortable adding your hands and making multiple decisions.

Just one last thing. You will play at some casinos where you can double only with a 10 or 11, or with a 9, 10, or 11 for your first two-card total. This is, of course, a chandelier rule for the casino, but you will sometimes have to play this way, so you might as well practice for it. If you don't practice with this rule, you will hear the dealer tell you what they told me: "Lady, you still can't double on that, just like the last godzillionth time I told you!" So if you draw an A,2 through an A,6 and cannot double, then you hit; if you draw an 8 or 9 and cannot double, then you hit; and if you draw an A,7 or an A,8 and cannot double, then you stand. The same logic actually applies to any three-card total which equals any of those mentioned here. I made up a house-rule sign by folding a small piece of poster board in half and writing "double allowed only on 10 or 11" on it. Then I sometimes set it on the table in front of me to force me to practice with this rule. It helped, so you might try it.

Okay, okay.... I asked you to place the discard pile on your upper left because that's where it will be in actual play, and in later chapters you will learn how glancing at discards helps you to win, so you might as well get used to placing it there. Now, are you happy? Good, now let's go on to...Las Vegas!

Practice Chart

Your Hand ▶ Dealer's Up-card ▶

Your Hand	Up	Hand	Up	Hand	Up	Hand	Up	Hand	Up	Hand	Up	Hand	Up	Hand	Up	Hand	Up	Hand	Up	Hand	Up
6,8	X	9,7	9	6,9	2	X,4	7	6,8	2	X,8	5	8,9	6	8,5	6	9,7	3	6,X	6	3,7	6
A,6	X	7,5	5	5,4	8	6,5	2	2,5	9	X,5	A	9,7	4	X,4	4	8,9	8	5,6	A	4,6	3
2,5	7	3,5	A	4,X	5	3,9	9	2,3	X	3,X	5	9,5	9	A,A	9	6,8	2	5,4	6	2,4	X
4,4	8	3,X	2	5,4	7	7,4	9	6,6	3	6,7	6	X,9	X	5,4	7	2,5	5	2,6	8	5,X	3
4,8	9	4,6	A	2,7	2	4,8	6	7,7	8	X,6	3	5,4	7	2,9	6	7,8	9	2,5	3	8,5	3
5,9	X	X,9	X	5,5	7	9,6	A	4,4	4	5,9	6	9,6	9	9,8	7	7,7	A	8,9	2	8,9	4
4,3	A	A,4	3	X,2	5	7,7	9	3,9	3	X,A	X	6,9	5	5,6	5	A,9	7	3,3	2	7,5	7
A,7	7	5,5	7	5,6	6	A,6	8	7,7	X	X,4	4	9,9	9	8,4	9	6,9	A	X,X	4	4,3	5
7,4	4	A,6	X	3,3	8	9,4	A	4,7	3	6,X	A	9,9	2	9,5	7	A,2	5	2,4	6	X,X	9
A,X	3	9,9	4	7,6	7	A,A	8	8,5	A	8,4	3	A,7	4	2,X	8	9,X	7	5,5	9	8,9	8
4,A	A	8,A	X	3,5	3	3,3	5	6,A	9	2,6	X	4,8	3	8,3	9	7,A	4	7,6	7	7,2	X
A,A	4	7,2	6	4,X	9	A,5	X	9,A	3	9,4	4	6,5	8	4,6	4	3,A	3	5,8	9	6,3	9
5,X	5	3,3	6	7,2	8	7,X	A	X,6	3	2,9	6	3,A	A	A,X	2	8,7	2	3,8	4	5,2	A
3,7	8	9,A	3	6,5	5	5,8	6	5,7	9	7,A	X	7,2	2	3,6	5	8,3	5	X,3	6	2,9	7
3,8	3	4,8	4	A,9	4	9,X	7	7,8	9	3,7	8	5,A	8	2,5	A	6,6	2	9,6	4	A,3	8
8,6	8	A,A	X	6,7	8	8,8	4	2,3	7	4,A	8	7,2	8	5,A	A	2,2	3	6,3	5	2,8	7
2,4	X	3,7	A	7,5	2	6,X	4	7,X	7	5,9	9	3,A	9	5,8	5	6,3	2	X,8	4	X,5	6
A,A	9	5,3	A	4,3	3	5,8	4	4,A	5	9,7	9	8,X	9	2,2	4	X,8	3	2,8	5	8,9	6
4,3	9	X,X	9	8,6	3	9,A	5	8,7	5	X,4	7	8,2	6	5,9	A	2,8	8	2,2	A	9,6	6
4,4	6	4,8	6	8,X	2	8,3	3	A,4	3	3,7	7	A,7	8	9,9	7	3,3	8	6,6	A	7,7	3
6,X	6	4,3	7	5,A	8	8,8	X	9,4	3	3,7	2	8,A	5	9,6	9	3,A	5	3,7	9	5,5	2
7,X	3	4,2	4	5,3	7	8,5	8	9,7	8	3,3	3	6,2	4	6,X	4	9,4	6	A,8	9	4,6	8

4,6	2	7,2	5	X,7	7	A,2	8	9,2	A	8,8	4	6,3	7	5,8	A	X,2	2	9,3	4
8,A	7	8,3	8	7,8	X	X,6	A	5,9	3	7,4	6	A,2	9	6,3	X	X,7	3	4,6	4
A,A	5	6,X	7	X,8	8	4,9	3	9,7	2	X,7	6	7,5	9	6,6	X	A,8	3	5,5	4
9,A	6	X,3	9	7,3	A	X,X	A	3,3	4	2,9	9	X,X	A	2,3	2	A,5	5	8,7	6
4,4	2	X,4	8	5,7	7	6,7	A	X,5	4	4,8	8	7,7	7	A,A	A	6,3	4	9,9	2
8,8	9	7,A	6	9,5	A	7,6	5	6,2	2	A,4	6	5,3	A	9,9	5	3,5	3	2,5	8
7,6	6	6,4	A	7,7	4	7,4	3	6,5	9	8,8	A	2,2	5	X,9	2	9,4	9	5,4	7
X,3	A	4,7	5	6,6	3	6,A	9	X,X	6	A,3	4	8,8	2	5,4	9	4,6	7	4,5	A
6,3	5	4,4	3	5,2	9	6,3	6	8,2	X	A,4	2	7,6	8	2,3	7	8,6	X	8,4	4
A,7	2	6,3	8	7,9	6	X,8	A	9,7	4	9,9	9	2,4	7	8,2	4	2,8	4	6,7	2
7,4	8	X,2	7	7,4	X	5,7	4	2,7	2	2,6	7	9,2	X	A,8	4	8,6	3	2,2	8
8,3	6	8,7	A	2,6	4	7,5	2	X,9	3	8,5	6	9,9	7	A,7	X	3,4	A	6,6	4
9,2	5	A,3	2	5,7	8	6,6	6	X,8	X	7,3	2	9,5	9	8,8	7	5,5	X	A,A	4
5,6	2	4,X	9	9,2	6	5,9	X	3,4	4	X,5	8	3,9	7	9,9	X	5,4	4	7,9	5
A,5	3	3,6	9	9,9	6	8,8	X	2,A	4	4,4	9	3,3	6	2,6	A	3,5	5	6,3	3
6,6	8	6,A	X	6,6	5	7,5	3	2,2	2	6,8	6	7,X	A	9,8	4	5,5	3	2,2	6
3,9	A	5,X	5	6,6	7	A,6	8	A,4	X	8,8	5	4,X	7	7,7	9	A,A	X	4,3	2
8,4	5	8,X	6	8,3	9	2,6	X	2,A	3	X,5	6	6,9	8	X,2	X	X,3	3	4,3	5
8,8	6	3,2	8	5,5	A	3,9	3	9,A	5	9,3	8	7,7	X	5,8	2	4,2	4	4,4	6
4,7	9	6,A	A	8,2	3	4,9	4	2,2	7	3,2	A	2,7	3	A,A	5	2,6	6	A,4	9
2,3	X	6,9	2	2,2	4	A,2	2	3,5	8	3,9	2	4,2	5	3,2	6	A,8	8	3,9	X
9,A	2	2,X	5	5,5	3	2,2	9	3,A	X	3,9	4	3,9	6	4,4	8	8,A	X	4,3	3
9,2	4	A,8	6	5,4	6	A,5	A	X,X	2	5,A	4	5,A	8	4,4	X	5,A	2	8,7	4
5,2	6	2,4	9	A,2	X	8,7	3	A,8	5	2,8	8	2,5	X	4,X	3	X,3	4	2,7	7
2,X	8	5,X	X	2,A	2	X,9	4	2,A	7	X,X	X	A,A	2	X,3	5	3,X	7	2,X	9
8,3	7	3,A	A	6,A	3	3,3	9	4,2	A	X,X	X	9,8	3	7,9	9	7,A	A	X,8	7
X,7	5	7,X	9	7,3	A	X,X	7	9,8	A	X,5	A	X,9	9	9,A	A	X,9	A	X,2	A

There is no other way to get the experience you need without "doing it." Count your money, make your reservations, and go! When you get there I want you to play blackjack under every set of casino conditions and rules that you can find. Play only at tables with $2 to $5 minimum bets, and don't bet more than twice the minimum. Split your money into day stakes, with $75 for your first day (partial day), $150 for the second day (full day), and $75 for your last day (partial day).

Play on the Strip, downtown, and at off-Strip casinos. Play at single-deck games, double-deck games, and six-deck games. Play at tables where you double on any first two cards, where you can double after splitting, and at tables where you are limited to doubling-down on 10 or 11. Play at full tables and alone (solo) against the dealer. Don't play longer than thirty minutes at any single table, don't take insurance, and *don't* play at any of the variation games, such as Double Exposure, or Triple Action. I want your money to last at least through the weekend!

I also want you to keep records during your trip. Tear out and make additional copies of the Casino Record Form in the back of this book. This form is strictly to encourage you to be observant. You will be surprised how quickly you forget which casino had the nice pit boss, or the rude dealer, or which one had the bad rules. Please keep the records faithfully. When you get back we will look at your records and discuss your experience in more detail.

Well, there's nothing left except to go! Have fun and good luck!

Chapter Overview

Look back at the expectation chart on page 29. Notice that your expected loss per hour as a typical player at a $5 table is $21, and with the basic system it is only $3. On average you will gain $18 per hour *just by learning the basics*. This is the largest single gain you will make during your learning process. So learn to deal with Aces, learn the Basic Chart, practice adding your hands, learn when to surrender, don't take insurance, and get some casino experience. You will recognize this on your own, but you *will* be ahead of 90 percent of all other players!

4

Analyze Yourself

I hear and I forget,
I see and I remember,
I do and I understand.

—CHINESE PROVERB

You're back! It sure doesn't take long to spend three days in Las Vegas.
Did you have fun? Did you win? I hope you enjoyed it, and I hope you
won, or at least didn't lose too much, because then you might not
recommend my book to your friends! Seriously, whether you won or lost
is not all that important at this point, but it may have had an impact on
your attitude, and your attitude definitely has an impact on your
blackjack future. I'm not a psychologist, but I have been there and I
know firsthand the ups and downs, lows and highs, frustration and
embarrassment. I also know the pure joy of playing winning blackjack. I
believe I can help you, so let's first take a look at your casino records.
You did keep them, didn't you?

The record keeping was strictly to keep you observant. Did you
notice any difference playing at casinos with fewer decks and better

rules where you had more options and opportunities? Did you notice that some casinos deal more cards (deeper card penetration) before shuffling? Was there a difference in playing at a full table and playing solo against the dealer? How did you feel playing against fast dealers? What about the grouchy dealers? Did you feel any difference between playing against male or female dealers? Was the atmosphere downtown different from that on the Strip? What about the floormen and pit bosses? Did they intimidate you? Did you drink, or play while you were tired? (If you went everywhere I asked you to, you *had* to have been tired.) Were you confident or unsure of yourself? Did you play perfect basic strategy, or did you make mistakes? Did you tip, and if so, how much? Were there significant distractions at any of the casinos? Did you find different table moods (intense, fun, sober, or loud)? As a female, were you treated as an equal to the male players? Last, did you sometimes win and other times lose? *All* of these factors have an impact on your overall success and satisfaction with blackjack. We won't attempt to analyze them individually, but spend some time talking about what happened.

If you made a few mistakes or felt unsure, it's nothing practice won't cure. If you felt intimidated or embarrassed, it's nothing experience won't cure. If you lost, it's nothing knowledge won't cure. If you felt men were treated differently than you, just *love* it, because this is your true strength! That factor is the key. All the problems you may have encountered are only inconveniences and are easy to overcome with time and determination.

You have worked hard learning how to deal with Aces, to quickly add your hands, and to make basic-play decisions. Your efforts have provided you with the ability to play almost even with the casinos. Now, building on your current, almost break-even basic strategy and advancing to a winning strategy will take an even more intense effort. Will it be worth it? That's for you to decide.

There are four methods of play which you can pursue, each with different efforts required, and each with different rewards. You have already been through the basics, and that is the first method. The second requires you to learn to count cards (this is actually fun) and bet according to the count. The third method requires you to count cards, bet according to the count, and play your hands differently based on the count. The fourth is partners. With this method you have to learn to play and bet according to the count, but someone else does the actual counting and sends you signals on which to base your betting and playing. Let's look more closely at these methods.

The basic method is strong and provides you with adequate knowledge to greatly reduce the casino advantage. You may have lost or you may have won on your trip, but with long play you will end up losing a little—about 0.5 percent of your action. This is a very small casino advantage, but it is still a *casino* advantage.

The count and count-dependent bet method is more effective and will provide you with the knowledge necessary to play *winning* blackjack. The time you spend learning this method is relatively brief, however, *practicing* enough to get good will take an investment—about one month of practice, forty-five minutes per day. This method of play will provide you with an approximate 0.75 percent advantage over the casino—and that's *good!*

There is an emotional trip you will take while counting cards that is difficult to explain, but I will try. The feeling revolves around knowing what is happening when no one else does. You will know in general terms what the composition of the decks are, and begin to mentally predict things happening, not only to your cards but to other players' cards and the dealer's. And your predictions will start to come true! A real high comes from that feeling. It is also a profitable feeling!

The third method involves not only counting cards and betting on a count-dependent basis, but also playing your hands differently. Combining count-dependent betting with count-dependent playing will provide you with an expectation of approximately 1.5 percent. The price you pay to learn the modifications to the Basic Chart, however, will take you about twice as long as it took to learn the original basic strategy. A small price to pay for doubling your advantage, don't you think?

The fourth method is sort of a combination and requires two people of almost the same level of expertise. One partner counts and sends signals to the other, who then bets and plays on a count-dependent basis. I am partial to this method because of the freedom it provides. It does, however, require that one person count and send signals. This is a little more difficult than just playing count strategy, but Steven hardly complains about it. It does take good teamwork, and you have to operate almost as one. It works extremely well for us, and if you have a willing partner it will work well for you.

The rewards of playing winning blackjack go way beyond the financial payoff. There is just something special about winning. I read a story that seemed to fit here. It might help you in your thought process.

A fortune-teller faced a particularly apprehensive but hopeful-looking customer. After careful thought the fortune-teller said, "You will be poor until you are forty, and this will make you unhappy."

Replied the client hopefully, "Then what?"

"Then you'll get used to it."

—AUTHOR UNKNOWN

Contrary to the client in the above story, I just couldn't accept losing as the predictable result of my gambling trips. Playing the slots, roulette, or keno was fun, but there was always something a little depressing about constantly coming home a loser. Winning really is a lot more fun! But I know that everyone is different. You may decide that you are satisfied with trimming the casino odds by using the basic strategy, or you may decide that you simply do not have the determination right now to go on to learning winning methods. If you decide to stop here, then I highly recommend that you purchase *Comp City* by Max Rubin. This is an outstanding guide to obtaining comps while you play basic-strategy blackjack, and is a must read. This book provides some extremely good tips for the card-counter as well, even if she doesn't want high exposure.

For the rest of you...well, you've made up your mind, so I'll help you all I can. Let's move on.

5

Count Your Cards—
Place Your Bet

Fantasize about possibilities but bet your money on
probabilities.

—STEVEN

"I can't do it! I am not like you!" I told Steven after he asked if I wanted
to learn. He retorted, "Don't say you *can't*. If you don't want to, just say
you don't want to, but don't say you *can't*." This conversation took place
one morning when I was making breakfast and he was practicing
counting. The process looked impossible. Steven continued, "Someday
you may want to, so set aside thirty minutes when you're ready and I'll
teach you." A year later, I was to find out that learning to count cards is
the easiest part of playing winning blackjack and was actually a lot of fun.

Counting

Steven uses a two-level system which he calls smooth and powerful. He
also keeps a side count of Aces and does this without crutches (stacking
little piles of chips and so forth). He doesn't look intense when he plays,
but he did when he first started. Sometimes I would deal to him when

he was practicing, and he would hold his forehead, move his lips, ask me to slow down (I didn't think I could go any slower), and would often toss his cards down and announce that he had lost the count. He struggled but he learned, and he remembered his mistakes. When he taught me it was much easier. He used a method that taught me to count in thirty minutes! It took a lot more practice to get good at it, but the learning was easy, and will be for you, too.

After I had played the basic strategy for a few trips and knew what was expected of me, we talked about which count method I should learn and use. It had to be user friendly, and I told him I wanted something that was "simple, sort of like you, Steven." (I told you I'd get even.) It also had to be smooth and strong.

During the trips I took to Las Vegas to get casino experience using the basic strategy, I really noticed the indifference with which women were treated. The pit bosses would pay attention to men at my table, but would mostly ignore me and the other women. I concluded that women were supposed to know a little, but not much. They were expected to be talking when they should be paying attention, and were expected to let intuition guide their betting and playing. I needed a count system which would allow me to play and win without having to be intense.

There are an incredible number of count systems available. The most comprehensive listing is included in Michael Dalton's book *Blackjack: A Professional Reference*. There are more than fifty systems included in his book. How do you choose one, particularly since everyone claims that theirs is the best?

Some of the methods are so complex that just learning one would turn any woman's hair gray. Fortunately, the statisticians made our work easier. Each method was analyzed, and some of the simpler ones were actually more efficient than the complex ones. Anyway, I chose a level one method, which is statistically strong, and is easy to learn and use. I can use the method and still act like a "female blackjack player"—you know, barely functional. While the strategies Steven developed were designed specifically for our partners game, they can be adapted quite well to the level one count method I chose.

The method I selected is called the Austin Method, the Einstein Method, or Hi-Opt 1. I think it was originally developed by either

Austin or Einstein and later named Hi-Opt 1. In any case, Lance Humble and Carl Cooper explain the system in wonderful form in *The World's Greatest Blackjack Book*. Their book is extremely informative and entertaining, and is definitely in my recommended-reading section.

Card-counting is a bit of a misnomer, because you really don't count the cards. The purpose is to determine, as the cards are played, the relative density of the cards left in the deck so you will know if you or the casino has the advantage. When there is an excess of high cards left in the deck, then you have the advantage; when there is an excess of low cards, the casino has it. When you have the advantage you will, of course, want to bet more. The count also influences the way you play your hands, i.e., a modification of the basic strategy, which you are now intimately familiar with.

At first I had no true deep-down confidence that card-counting would really work. I just didn't understand it, and maybe I still don't, but most of the reference books include sections explaining the statistical significance of removing various cards from play. If you just have to know why it works, then by all means expand your blackjack library. The proof to me came from the cash in my pocketbook!

Determining the density of various cards in the deck is accomplished by assigning a plus (+) or minus (−) value to the most important cards and keeping a running count of these as you see them. Sounds hard? Well, it's really not. Take about thirty seconds and memorize the count method shown in the following chart (10-value cards are shown as an X).

Count Method

Card Value	2	3	4	5	6	7	8	9	X	A
Count Value	0	+1	+1	+1	+1	0	0	0	−1	0

When I first saw this I wondered: If ten-value cards are better for the player and low cards are better for the casino, why are the good cards given a minus value while the bad cards are given a plus value? It seemed backward to me. Well, you have to remember that you are counting them as they *leave* the deck. So if a card which is good for you leaves the deck, then that's good for the casino (and that's bad for you), so you give it a minus value. When cards that are good for the casino leave, then it's good for you and you give them a plus value. Makes sense.

Have you memorized the chart? If not, go back and look at it. You may have noticed that you only have to count 3s, 4s, 5s, 6s, and ten-value cards. When you are counting, ignore the others; they count as 0. In a single deck, there are four 3s, four 4s, four 5s, four 6s, and sixteen ten-value cards (four each of 10s, Jacks, Queens, and Kings). Count them; there are sixteen minus cards and sixteen plus cards. But let's go on before I use up your thirty minutes.

Step One

Get your deck of cards and separate thirteen of them into a pile as follows: one each of 2, 3, 4, 5, 6, 7, 8, 9, 10, Jack, Queen, King, and Ace.

Step Two

Shuffle the little deck and turn the cards up, one at a time, and say the count value for each card. If you turn up a 5, say, "plus one,"; if you turn up a ten-value card, say, "minus one," and so forth. Do this until you no longer have to look at the chart for help. It should take you about ten minutes.

Step Three

Shuffle the little deck again and turn the cards up, one at a time, but this time keep a "running count" of the pluses and minuses. The following chart is an example of how to keep the count. The left-hand column gives the cards as you may turn them over; the next column shows the count value; the next column shows the running count; and the right-hand column shows the math.

You will notice that the last running count total is 0. It only makes sense, because there are four −1 cards and four +1 cards in your thirteen-card deck, and the rest count as 0. Practice going through your cards and keeping a running count until you get the hang of it, probably about twenty minutes. If you count them and don't come up with 0 at the end, it means you made a mistake. Keep trying.

Counting Example

Card	Count Value	Running Count	Math
6	+1	+1	
9	0	+1	(+1+0=+1)
3	+1	+2	(+1+1=+2)
A	0	+2	(+2+0=+2)
10	−1	+1	(+2−1=+1)
5	+1	+2	(+1+1=+2)
J	−1	+1	(+2−1=+1)
2	0	+1	(+1+0=+1)
8	0	+1	(+1+0=+1)
K	−1	0	(+1−1=0)
7	0	0	(0+0=0)
Q	−1	−1	(0−1=−1)
4	+1	0	(−1+1=0)

Now you know how to count cards! It will take some time to get good at it, but practicing is actually fun. When you get to where you can count the small deck with few mistakes, start turning over the cards two at a time. Counting this way will be required in actual play, so practice it. It won't take long to get comfortable with that process, probably about an hour. After you have completed that, shuffle your thirteen cards back into the full deck and practice with it for a while.

Next, shuffle two or more decks together and do the same thing. Counting more than one deck is exactly the same as counting one deck, you just don't get to rest as often.

I test myself by putting one card aside face down, and after I count the remaining deck, I predict what that card is. If I end the count with a +1, then I know the card has to be a −1 card (ten-value card) for the count to zero-out; if I end with a 0, then I know the card has to be a 0 card (2, 7, 8, 9, or an Ace); if I end with a −1, then the card has to be a +1 (3, 4, 5, or 6). This little game is fun, and is an excellent way to test yourself. Practice this for a while before you go on.

Interconnectivity

All right ladies, if you drink it's time to have a toddy. Celebrate your progress, and prepare yourself for the next step. If you don't drink, then say a few kind words to the blackjack goddess. You've come a long way, but the next step will test your determination! This step will also be the first *true* test of your knowledge of the Basic Chart. If you know the chart like your own name, then it will be a little easier, but if you don't...well, you hardly have a chance. I am serious, so be honest with yourself! If you are uncertain about it, go back to Chapter 3 right now and review the chart. I don't mean to scare you (like hell I don't!), but I really want you to succeed!

You have analyzed yourself and have made up your mind that you want to become a *winning* blackjack player. To do this you will have to start thinking and remembering on three different levels. One will be from your subconscious, the basic strategy (which is etched there, like your name); the second is the process of adding your hands, which quickly becomes almost unconscious; and the last is the count. Any one of these is easy; actually, two of them aren't bad, but combining the three is a true mental exercise. Don't give up. I didn't, and I'm living proof that we "stupid" females can do it. So can you, and you start here. Get your full deck of cards and play with the ghost dealer (don't forget to put your discard pile on your upper left). Play both hands just like you did when you were in the final stages of learning the basic strategy, but this time maintain the count. Count the cards as you see them (the dealer's up-card, your two cards, any hits you take, the dealer's down-card, and any hits the dealer takes). At first it will seem impossible, but keep trying and you will discover that your brain will actually start to accept the challenge and rise to meet it! Repetition is the real secret here, so practice for at least fifteen minutes, at least three times a day. After a few days, try playing *two* hands against the dealer. In about two weeks you will be gaining some confidence, and after a month you will actually have it together.

I know it has been hard, but now you have the necessary knowledge to reverse the casino odds. Remember Oprah's credo, "Knowledge is power." Well, it's time to put your power to work. Decisions on betting, playing your hands, taking insurance, and surrendering, will now become count-dependent.

A Sip at a Time

Before we go on, I have to expose you to the concept of "true count" (no, it doesn't mean you have made mistakes). This was a confusing concept to me at first, but I finally got it, and developed a way to deal with it in little "SIPS" (significant points).

I will use two extremes to demonstrate the concept. First, assume that you have a +5 count after the first five cards were dealt in a two-deck game (say a 3, 4, 5, 6, and 4 were dealt). All the ten-value cards remain, thirty-two of them, but there are ninety-nine cards left to be played in that two-deck game, so only 32 percent of the remaining cards are ten-value. Now assume that the dealer has dealt almost to the bottom of the deck and there are only five cards left (I told you it would be an extreme example), and your count is still +5. Now all of the remaining cards, 100 percent, are ten-value! Quite a difference with the same +5 count, and also quite deceiving!

Most blackjack authorities would now want you to learn how to convert to the true count by dividing the running count by the number of decks, or half-deck, left to be played. Steven constantly makes corrections to a half-deck standard, but he tells me that adding that step would make it more difficult to act the way I am expected to act: I would have to concentrate so hard that the pit boss might notice I'm *not* stupid. Counting, adding, and playing my hands is enough to handle without adding in another step. To tackle this problem, we established significant decision points—SIPS—complete with betting and playing strategies.

We initially developed this for use when we were playing partners, but it worked so well that I adapted it for use when playing alone. Since you have been counting cards with your ghost dealer, you have noticed that sometimes the count is good for you and sometimes bad, but how good is good, and how bad is bad? I use +5 and −5 for the significant points. Any count above 0 is good, and any count above +5 (+SIPS) is real good. Any count below 0 is bad, and any count below −5 (−SIPS) is real bad. Sound arbitrary? It's really not, because the advantage, or disadvantage, at the SIPS are significant, and therefore justify different betting and playing decisions.

Now, back to my example where the same +5 count was misleading you. To compensate, the SIPS have to change (it won't always be a +5 or −5), depending on how many decks are left to be played. When one deck is left, the new SIPS are actually equal in advantage, or disadvantage, to the +5 or −5 count. It sounds complicated, but it's really not. The following chart will show what the +5 or −5 becomes (correct SIPS) with various amounts of decks left to be played.

SIPS Chart

Decks Remaining	SIPS
7	(+ or −) 35
6	(+ or −) 30
5	(+ or −) 25
4	(+ or −) 20
3	(+ or −) 15
2	(+ or −) 10
1-1/2	(+ or −) 8
1	(+ or −) 5
1/2	(+ or −) 3

For example, when the count reaches +20 with about four decks to be played, it is running very much in the player's favor. If it were at +10 with two decks left, then it is still significantly in the player's favor. If the count were at −15 with three decks left, or at −5 with one deck left, then the casino advantage is significant. *Remember, the SIPS are always equal to 5 (+ or −) with one deck left to be played.*

Learning the SIPS chart is not difficult. Notice that the SIPS are in multiples of five for each full deck remaining. It is 5 for one deck, 10 for two decks, 15 for three decks, and so forth. If you remember that, then you will only have to memorize two numbers! The SIPS for one and a half decks remaining is 8 (+ or −), and it is 3 (+ or −) with a half deck remaining. See, it's not so bad.

Determining how many cards remain to be played could have been a problem, but you faithfully placed your practice cards in a discard pile at your upper left. Here's why. Estimates of how many decks, or partial decks, are in the dealer's hand, or how many are in the shoe, will often be deceiving. Cards in the dealer's hand are partially hidden, and cards in the shoe are tilted. So forget trying to watch the cards remaining and concentrate on how many have been played. The cards which have been played are neatly stacked in the discard tray. All you have to do is glance at the discards to make your decisions.

Practice using the discard pile to estimate how many cards remain. First you have to remember how many decks are in play, i.e., one, two, four, six, or eight. For example, if you are at a two-deck game and one deck is in the discard bin, one deck is left to be played. Referring to the chart, you'll see that your SIPS with one deck remaining is +5 or −5. This is where it is real good or real bad. If one and a half decks are in the discard tray, then a half deck is left to be played, and +3 or −3 is your SIPS. Practice by putting a half deck and a full deck beside your discard pile to use as reference points. Use the SIPS Chart as shown. Count down by whole decks until there are two decks left to be played, then use the new SIPS for every half deck. Again, practice is what makes it easy, so practice for a while and then we'll go on. While you are practicing, remember the old saying, "Everything is hard before it is easy."

Betting

How a player bets her money is the first thing a casino boss will look for to determine if she poses a threat to the casino bank. Fortunately, they pay much less attention to us (or at least to the way we play blackjack) than they do to male players. They really believe that it's highly unlikely women can play a winning game. Now it's time to combine your ability with their chauvinism. However, use caution. Don't attract attention to yourself because of the way you bet. Remember, what you want is their money—*not* their respect.

Anytime the count is above 0 you have the advantage, and it justifies a bet above the minimum. When the count reaches + SIPS, it justifies your maximum bet. When the count is at 0 or below, you would prefer not to bet anything, because the casino has the advantage. However, if you are going to sit at the table you have to bet something, so keep at the minimum allowed. (There are actually a few ways to bet nothing when the deck is negative, and these will be discussed in chapter 8.) I use a bet spread of one to eight units, and the following chart shows how I bet depending on the count.

Count-Dependent Betting

Count	Bet
0 or less	1 unit
+1 up to +SIPS	2 to 4 units
+SIPS or more	5 to 8 units

How quickly a player raises or lowers her bet is the real trigger which alerts a casino boss that something might be going on. I "attempt" to bet one unit when the count is 0 or below, two to four units when the count is plus, and five to eight units when the count is at +SIPS or greater. I said "attempt" because I never raise my bet from my minimum to my maximum, nor do I lower it from my maximum to my minimum, in a single hand.

For example, if I bet one unit on a minus count, and during that hand the count reached +SIPS (this happens, particularly at a full table), I would then bet three units, regardless of whether I won or lost the last hand. If I win that hand, I will parlay (six units now) and add two more chips just for luck. That puts me at my maximum. If I had lost the prior hand, so that now I couldn't parlay, I would then have bet four units and hope for the best. Reducing your bet from maximum to minimum works in much the same way. Don't drop your bet from eight units to one when the count goes from +SIPS to minus. That would be like dropping an armload of dishes and hoping no one noticed.

I have seen men raise and lower their bets in a fashion as moderate as mine and immediately catch heat from the pit boss, so stay alert. There are no rigid guidelines to follow when betting, just use your common sense and be aware of any attention you might be getting. If you suspect that they suspect, then leave. Don't chance it. I have left only two casinos because I thought they suspected something, but remember, if you do get caught and kicked out, you can't play in that casino for a long time—and that's not good! Also, the bad news could get worse! Suppose you were kicked out of Sam's Town Casino in Las Vegas. The Boyd Gaming Corporation, which also own the California,

Eldorado, Fremont, Jokers Wild, and the Stardust own Sam's Town. Do they share information on card-counters? You can bet on that!

I do have a flexible rule that I follow just to keep me from getting too smug, and that is to stay no longer than one hour in any single casino. You are not likely to catch any heat in one hour, even if you are winning big. Winning will be looked upon as just a "streak of luck"—but don't push *your* luck. If you stayed, say, for two hours and were winning, then the bosses might start watching you closely, or they might even ask the eye-in-the-sky to track your play. It's not worth taking a chance. I did say, though, that this is flexible. I have played at tables where the other players were betting big and having a loud and wild good time. Under these conditions, I have truly been invisible and have stayed and played for hours. Again, common sense is the key.

I need to point out that I know two very good female blackjack players who disagree with me on the amount of time to play in each casino. The first believes that there is currently no reason to worry. She finds a casino she likes and plays there for days. She is good at the game and doesn't believe she has ever been under suspicion. The other believes I am too liberal. She's a dealer at a casino in Laughlin, Nevada and plays blackjack two days a week in Las Vegas. She is very good, but admits that her exposure to pit bosses may be making her paranoid. Nevertheless, she believes you should never stay longer than thirty minutes in any casino. She also says, "You have to get really good at acting really dumb."

Insurance

You can now start taking insurance anytime you are at +SIPS. Remember that insurance isn't insurance; it is strictly a side bet and has nothing to do with your hand, or the moon, or the stars above. You are simply placing a bet that the dealer has a ten-value card under an Ace showing. When there are enough ten-value cards among those remaining so that you will win more money than you lose, then you place your bet. That happens at +SIPS.

Even Money

You will occasionally be dealt a blackjack when the dealer has an Ace showing. In this situation, if the count is at +SIPS you can either take insurance or ask for even money. Most casinos allow this, and will simply pay you an amount equal to your bet (not 3 for 2), before they check their hole card. Asking for even money at +SIPS has the same win expectation as the insurance bet.

Surrender

Remember, some casinos let you surrender (forfeit half your bet)—a good alternative to losing it all. Taking advantage of the surrender option is now count-dependent. The following table shows when you should surrender.

Surrender

Your Hand	Dealer's Up-card		
	9	**X**	**A**
14	+SIPS	+	+SIPS
15	+	+	+
16*	+	+	+

*Split if it is an 8,8 against a 9.

Chapter Overview

Learning to count cards really is easy and fun. Learning the SIPS chart and to accurately estimate the number of cards remaining isn't bad, but the memorization and repetition is a little boring. The biggest problem you are going to encounter is combining everything you are learning. Counting the cards, maintaining the count, playing your hands, and applying SIPS to your betting is a real mental trip. As you are trying to put all this together, you will probably say "that °&%#@ Angie." You may even, as I did, declare that it's impossible, that it just "can't be done." Well, it can be done—and you can do it. Just don't give up, it will come together. When it does the casinos will have good reason to fear you, but of course they won't, because they don't think you are capable. Oh…don't forget to apologize for all the bad things you said about me!

6

Go All the Way

Life consists not of holding good cards, but in playing
those you do hold well.

—Unknown Philosopher

There I was, face to face with what could have been one of the most
intimidating situations known to women. One wrong move and I would
be totally vulnerable. Men surrounded me, and I would soon have to
make a decision that would affect them all. I had been there before, and
I knew that no matter what happened, they weren't going to like it.
While they were debating the situation, I was reflecting on how I had
gotten myself into this wonderful mess.

It started earlier that day when Steven decided to go the Tropicana
while I went Christmas shopping at the Fashion Show Mall. The stores
had unique merchandise, which was hard to find back home, but the
shopping had not taken as long as I thought it would, and I was anxious
to get back to the blackjack tables. I soon found myself in Harrah's, one
of my favorite casinos. Its rules were liberal, and I liked the atmosphere.
I was hoping to find a quiet table, but that was not to be. It was a busy
weekend and I soon discovered that the only seat available was at a $25
minimum, two-deck game, with all men playing at the table. I really
hadn't planned on involving myself in the pressure of a high-stakes

game, but it appeared to be this or nothing, and I just wasn't excited about the nothing option. Steven and I usually play the high-stakes games as partners, but he wasn't there, so I pulled out the chair, put $500 on the table, and said, "I hope you gentlemen don't mind if I join you."

I could almost hear their stares. They looked at me, then at each other with a look that implied, "Oh crap, she'll probably screw up everybody's hands." I had seen it plenty of times before, but they tried to be nice, and one of them even said, "Nah, we don't mind, sit down." I thought that was awfully nice of him, because I was already sitting down, and had already bought in. "Thank you," I said, "I hope you don't mind if I ask a lot of questions, because I haven't played this game in a while." Now I could hear their moans. One of the men was playing a large stack of black chips and he pulled them back, reducing his bet to one green chip. This could actually be fun, I thought to myself.

I joined the game in the middle of a deck, so I bet small, played basic strategy, and took advantage of the time to get acquainted. By the time the dealer shuffled I had learned their names and where they were from. They were warming up some. I guess they could see that at least I knew how to add my hands, and hit, stand, or double-down. Colorado Tom was back to betting black chips. I smiled.

Oregon Ed, on my left, was an aggressive player who liked to bet big, and double and split a lot. California Bill was on my right, and he was conservative—a perfect situation for me. Depending on the answer I wanted, I had the option of asking either of them for advice. I could bet big or small. I could double or hit. I could do almost anything, and one of them would indicate it was the right thing. However, they both agreed that I shouldn't have split the ten-value cards on one hand, and when I won, they agreed that I was just lucky. Ed said, "Listen, little lady, you never split a pat hand; you won't be lucky on those every time."

On one hand I drew a 9 and 2 against a dealer's 7. They both told me to double, but I knew I couldn't. The deck was not right. So I said, "My intuition tells me not to this time." I took two hits and won, but I wouldn't have if I had doubled. They started calling me the Lucky Lady. At one point, Ed and Bill got into a loud argument about how I should play a hand, and Bill said, "Look at her stack of chips, maybe you should be taking advice from her!" Ed struck back, "Oh bull, she got most of it 'cause she was bettin' so much when she got those blackjacks." I didn't

like the conversation, and looked out of the corner of my eye to see if
the pit boss was listening. He was, and he was walking from his podium
to our table. Uh, oh! He scanned the table, paying particular attention
to my pile of chips, and said, "Guys, we all know there's nothing luckier
than a hot woman." They all laughed, and although I caught the double
meaning, I smiled like I thought it was funny. I was all right—the pit
boss suspected nothing.

Ed shook me back to my immediate predicament when he said,
"Lady, don't you dare take the dealer's bust card." Bill agreed. "Stand
on that and let the dealer bust." I was holding a total of 12 and the
dealer had a 4 showing. Now, in many of these situations you should
stand, but the deck was poor, mostly low cards left. I knew what I had to
do. I also knew I would have to leave after this hand, no matter how it
turned out. The men had all done the wrong thing: they all had huge
bets out on a very negative deck; about $3,000 was combined in their
betting circles. They were all looking at me, and the dealer was getting
impatient. "Lady, what are you going to do?" I swallowed, scratched my
cards on the felt, and said, "I want a hit." The dealer turned up my next
card, a 2. Now I had 14 against a dealer's 4. Oh God, I had to take
another card! Colorado Tom had the largest bet out, probably $800, and
his look could have killed as I asked for another hit. A 4. Now I had 18,
and stood. The dealer had a 3 in the hole, hit with a 7, and then busted
with an 8. He shook his head and said, "If she hadn't taken both those
cards, I would have made 20 and you all would have lost."

Now you would have thought that everyone would have been pleased
that I had saved the table and their money, but they weren't. Ed said,
"Lady, you're the luckiest person alive, cause that was the dumbest card
playing I have ever seen!" They all agreed. Yes, it was time for me to
leave, but I was smiling inside as I stuffed handfuls of black chips into
my purse. It was one of my better days.

That day at Harrah's was fun, and it is fun telling you about it, but,
what's more important is that it provides me with a good example of
what a big role playing your hands based on the count can play. The
basic strategy teaches you to play your hand when you know nothing
other than your hand and the dealer's up-card. By card-counting you
now know a lot more. You know when there are more ten-value cards
remaining, or when there are more low cards than normal. You will now

put this knowledge to work for you by modifying the basic strategy to make it count-dependent.

When there are more ten-value cards than normal you are not going to want to hit as much because your odds of busting would be greater, but you will want to double-down more often on certain hands. With more low cards in the deck you are going to hit more and double-down less. The count will also influence the way you split pairs.

The Count-Dependent Playing Chart is shown in three sections on the following pages, again with the player's hand down the left-hand column and the dealer's up-card across the top row. It reveals the modifications for plus and minus, and for + SIPS and − SIPS. The basic chart is shown across from the player's hand, and any count-dependent changes are indicated. SIPS is designated with an asterisk (*).

As you look at the charts in all their dull and boring charm, please keep in mind that learning them will double your odds against the casino. After Steven and I first put the count-dependent playing charts together I was completely intimidated. I was overwhelmed as I looked at them, but I studied and Steven quizzed me. It was frustrating, but after three weeks of misery I had them etched in my brain alongside the Basic Chart. In retrospect, those three weeks really weren't so bad, and it was well worth it!

To assist you in learning and understanding the charts, I have pulled out the following row (player's hand against dealers' up-cards) for explanation.

Your			Dealer's Up-card							
Hand	2	3	4	5	6	7	8	9	X	A
	−H	−H	−*H	−*H	−*H	+*D				
9	D	D	D	D	D		H	H	H	H

Notice that the basic decisions are shown directly across from the 9, and any count-dependent changes are above them. Again, SIPS is designated with an asterisk (*). Learn them in the following manner:

Nine against dealer's 2: Double, but if the count is minus, then hit.
Nine against dealer's 3: Double, but if the count is minus, then hit.

Nine against dealer's 4: Double, but if the count is −SIPS, then hit.
Nine against dealer's 5: Double, but if the count is −SIPS, then hit.
Nine against dealer's 6: Double, but if the count is −SIPS, then hit.
Nine against dealer's 7: Hit, but if the count is +SIPS, then double.

Explanation:

Nine against a dealer's 2 or 3: When the count is minus, you will hit instead of following the basic decision to double. With a minus count you are less likely to draw a ten-value card, and the dealer is more likely to draw low cards to make a hand without busting.

Nine against a dealer's 4, 5, or 6: When the count is −SIPS, you will hit instead of following the basic decision to double. With a −SIPS count, there are an abundance of low cards remaining. You are much more likely to draw a low card than a ten-value card, and the dealer is much more likely to make a hand without busting.

Nine against a dealer's 7: When the count is +SIPS, you will double instead of following the basic decision to hit. In this case, there is an abundance of ten-value cards in the remaining cards and you are much more likely to draw to a 19. The dealer is likely to have a 17. So double your bet and double your winnings!

Learning the charts will be similar to learning the basics. There is no easy way. There are tear-out copies in the back of the book, and you may want to make flash cards. Use the practice chart in chapter 3 to test yourself.

Count-Dependent Playing (8 Through 16)

Your Hand	Dealer's Up-card									
	2	3	4	5	6	7	8	9	X	A
8				+*D	−H					
	H	H	H	H	D	H	H	H	H	H
9	−H	−H	−*H	−*H	−*H	+*D				
	D	D	D	D	D	H	H	H	H	H
10						−*H	−*H	−H	+*D	+*D
	D	D	D	D	D	D	D	D	H	H
11							−*H	−*H	−*H	−H
	D	D	D	D	D	D	D	D	D	D
12	+*S	+S	−H	−*H	−*H					
	H	H	S	S	S	H	H	H	H	H
13	−*H	−*H	−*H	−*H	−*H					
	S	S	S	S	S	H	H	H	H	H
14	−*H	−*H	−*H							
	S	S	S	S	S	H	H	H	H	H
15	−*H	−*H							+*S	
	S	S	S	S	S	H	H	H	H	H
16								+*S	+S	
	S	S	S	S	S	H	H	H	H	H

The asterisk symbol (*) signifies SIPS

Count-Dependent Playing (A,2 Through A,9)

Your Hand	**Dealer's Up-card**									
	2	3	4	5	6	7	8	9	X	A
A,2	H	H	−H / D	−H / D	−*H / D	H	H	H	H	H
A,3	H	+*D / H	−H / D	−*H / D	−*H / D	H	H	H	H	H
A,4	H	+*D / H	−H / D	−*H / D	D	H	H	H	H	H
A,5	H	+*D / H	−*H / D	−*H / D	D	H	H	H	H	H
A,6	−H / D	−*H / D	−*H / D	D	D	H	H	H	H	H
A,7	+D / S	−*S / D	−*S / D	D	D	S	S	H	H	+S / H
A,8	S	+*D / S	+*D / S	+*D / S	−S / D	S	S	S	S	S
A,9	S	S	S	+*D / S	+*D / S	S	S	S	S	S

The asterisk symbol (*) signifies SIPS

Count-Dependent Playing (Pairs)

Your Hand	2	3	4	5	6	7	8	9	X	A
A,A	Sp	Sp	Sp	Sp	Sp	Sp	Sp	Sp	Sp	−*H Sp
2,2	H	−H Sp	−*H Sp	Sp	Sp	Sp	H	H	H	H
3,3	H	+*Sp H	−H Sp	−*H Sp	Sp	Sp	H	H	H	H
6,6	−H Sp	−*H Sp	−*H Sp	−*H Sp	Sp	H	H	H	H	H
7,7	Sp	Sp	Sp	Sp	Sp	Sp	H	H	−H S	H
8,8	Sp	Sp	Sp	Sp	Sp	Sp	Sp	Sp	+*S Sp	Sp
9,9	−*S Sp	−*S Sp	−*S Sp	−*S Sp	−*S Sp	S	Sp	Sp	S	S
X,X	S	S	S	+*Sp S	+*Sp S	S	S	S	S	S

The asterisk symbol (*) signifies SIPS

Aces

Aces are a problem, not only to beginning blackjack players but also to mathematicians, statisticians, and computers. We all know that Aces are good when they come to us with a ten-value card on our first two, but what about when you double-down on an 11? Sometimes they are good and sometimes they are bad; sometimes they are low and sometimes they are high. No wonder they cause everyone so much trouble. However, they are very important to the game (both in betting and playing), and the only accurate way to use them is to keep a separate count of only Aces. Go ahead and say it, "Yeah, right." I felt the same way until I did it.

I decided to let my feet keep the score! My left foot keeps track of the first four Aces, while my right foot keeps track of the second four. If I am at a six-deck game, I use a chip to signify that eight Aces have fallen and I start over. Once you decide to try this, or a method of your own, be sure that it is undectable.

What to do with this newfound information now becomes the challenge. When Aces are balanced there are, of course, one in every thirteen cards, two in every half-deck, four in every deck, eight in two decks, and so forth. It is when they are out of balance that their importance climbs. I don't start adjusting the way I bet or play until there are 50 percent more or less than a balanced ratio of Aces left to be played.

For example, we are at a two-deck game. One deck resides in the discard tray, but only two Aces have been played. Therefore there are six in the remaining deck (50 percent more than normal). Since Aces are good for betting purposes, I would then raise my bet above what I would usually do. In fact, if the count were plus, I would treat it like it was at + SIPS, but with an excess of Aces, I would not double-down on an 11 if the dealer had a 7 or higher showing. Why not? Because I would be more likely to draw an Ace to my 11 and end up with a 12 (ugh!). On the other hand, I would double-down more often on a 10 than I normally would. Why? You figure that one out.

Let's assume we're in the same two-deck game but more Aces than normal have fallen and only two are left in the last deck to be played. In this case, I would reduce my bet and double on an 11 more often than the chart would tell me to, and less often on a 10. Counting Aces is not hard, and it gives you a feel for what is going on. I highly recommend it.

Partners

I have become a true believer in blackjack partners. I play with Steven as my partner, but it would work just as well if my partner was another woman, or a group of women. When Steven and I play partners, he does all the counting and sends me signals that tell me if the count is + or −, or if it has reached + SIPS or − SIPS. This leaves me totally free to act however I want, but always in a way that would prove that I am not counting. I may talk nonstop to the lady sitting next to me; I may "forget" to play my cards; and I may sometimes "forget" to bet. I may talk to the dealer about a show at the Mirage, or to the pit boss about the casino expansion. I may—well, the list is endless. What it really does is let me act like a female player (how they *expect* a female player to act) without the burden of counting the cards myself. I'm still winning, but it looks like the dumb luck of a friendly but not too-bright woman. It is a terrific way to play.

If you decide to try this, then the signals become critical. You have to develop signals that are natural to you and your partner and undetectable by the casino personnel. It took Steven and me a good while to work this out. Start by using everything available to you (chips, drinks, hands, fingers, arms, head, knees, or anything else). Whatever you decide to use, be sure it feels and looks natural, then practice until it's undetectable. *You don't want to get caught doing this!* We have several different sets of signals we use, and before taking them to a casino we tested them all at home by having one of our high school kids deal to us, with instructions to watch for any signals we were sending. If, after one hour of dealing, they couldn't detect our signals we adopted them (the signals, that is, the kids came with the territory).

Playing Partners With "Iowa"

Sometimes other players benefit from our partners game. This happened to us once when we were playing alone at a $10, two-deck game at the Excalibur. We had been there for a while, and things were running pretty neutral. We were talking about taking a breakfast break.

Just as we were about to leave, an elderly gentleman walked up to the table and asked if he could join us. Of course we welcomed him, and he took the spot on the other side of Steven. Since it was my job to do the talking I found out that he was from a farm in Iowa and two years prior had lost his wife. Las Vegas was his escape. He was also very timid and conservative (he almost left when he realized it was a $10 table, because he usually played at $2 tables). I immediately liked this country gentleman.

Then the deck went positive. I did not know how positive until later, but I had the + SIPS signal and raised my bet accordingly. I was also counting Aces; none had fallen. Our elderly friend ("Iowa") had won the prior hand and had partially parlayed. He now had $15 in the betting circle—something he said he never did. I was happy for him. I drew a two-card 20, Steven drew a three-card 18, and Iowa drew a two-card 20, all this to the dealer's three-card 19. Everybody won except Steven. Oh, well. Still a + SIPS signal, so things were still good.

Steven began talking to our friend, something rare during our partners game. He was telling him that he should "let it ride," because he had to gamble some if he wanted to make any money playing blackjack. Now I knew Steven would not say this if things were not good (better than good). He was talking to Iowa, but I knew he was *addressing his comments to me!* Again I raised my bet to my maximum. Iowa had $30 in the circle and Steven had $15, his cover bet. The dealer turned a 9 up, I drew another two-card 20, Steven busted (poor guy), and Iowa drew an A,5.

Iowa, obviously worried, asked Steven what he should do. Steven looked at his cards, shook his head, and told him he had to hit because a 16 against a 9 isn't good. The card came down—a 10. Shoot! A hard 16 with a high count against a dealer's 9. This is where Steven usually says, "You lean back, face east, say a few words to the blackjack goddess, cross your fingers, close your eyes, and stand." Instead, Steven told him, "You have to stand or else you'll bust like I did." He didn't explain why it was okay to stand on a hard 16 but not on a soft 16, but Iowa must have been too nervous to notice. He stood and the dealer turned a 5 out of the hole for a 14, hit with an 8, and busted!

We were cheering and laughing with excitement—except Steven. He was again telling Iowa that he should "let it all ride." Farmers gamble against the weather, crop prices, and bankers all the time, but I could tell this was a bit much for our friend. Steven finally told him, "With your kind of luck you shouldn't hesitate at all." Iowa looked at his chips and reluctantly, *very* reluctantly, let the $60 ride. Now, Steven and I play together a lot, so I knew something spectacular was going on. I maxed out my bet and added another chip, just for luck. Steven lost the last bet, so he was standing on his cover bet. He looked at my bet and gave me a nod that only I would notice.

Please deal, please deal, I was thinking, and hoping my mental telepathy would work. There was almost a deck and a half in the discard tray, and it was about time for a shuffle. The dealer was a young man, and he glanced at the cards in his hand. Decision time. I slid a red chip to the top of my betting circle and said, "You've been awfully nice and we're going to eat after this hand, so if I win, you win."

Butterflies. The deal? Yes! Blackjack to me, 20 to Steven, and blackjack to our friend from Iowa! Wow! The dealer had a 20, so Steven pushed (better than his last two hands), but I won pretty big and our friend now had $150 in his circle. Iowa looked like he was in shock!

We made our "hungry" noises and announced it was time for breakfast. We wished Iowa the best of luck and headed upstairs to the coffee shop. As we found the entry to the cafe, Iowa showed up and asked if we were going back to the tables after we ate. We explained that we had plans to casino hop and asked if he wanted to join us for breakfast. He graciously declined, saying he had already eaten and was going back to the tables. He apologized for not thanking us properly when we left the table, but said he had never been that lucky before. Lucky, indeed. Steven told me over breakfast that the count had reached almost a +20, and we both knew the only Ace that had fallen was the one Iowa had drawn on the A,5 hand. Sometimes the blackjack goddess is on your side!

I often think of this gentleman from Iowa and hope he is still lucky and doing as well against the weather as he did at the blackjack table that day.

Chapter Overview

Learning to play your hands based on the count is very important, but it is really dry stuff. There is just no way that I can make it exciting.

However, you will find that applying that knowledge at the tables is exciting—and profitable! Learning to keep a separate count of Aces is actually fairly easy, and is kind of fun—if you let your feet do all the work! Using the Aces side-count provides more accurate information for betting and playing—and, more profit! Playing partners is an option, but if you have a willing partner I highly recommend it. It's a great way for women to play their game.

7

You Gotta Pay to Play

The way I see it, if you want the rainbow, you gotta put up with the rain.

—Dolly Parton

Now that I am teaching you to play winning blackjack, I want you to learn how to lose. This is a horrible contradiction, but unfortunately, it is necessary.

Earlier, I asked you to establish a gambling fund and to never gamble with money you couldn't afford to lose. This is very important, because even when you are playing a winning strategy you can still have a lengthy losing streak. I don't want to get carried away with this discussion, but it can happen. I have had losing sessions, losing days, and even losing trips.

Everytime I think about losing, one fateful trip to Las Vegas always comes to mind. Steven and I had been there for two days and were down about $400 between us. On an average trip we would have been considerably ahead at this point, but not this time. The third morning of the trip found us sitting at a $25 table at the Luxor. About fifteen minutes after we got there the deck went positive. Then I bet $150 and drew a good double-down hand. I slid another $150 into my circle, and lost it! The next two hands were repeats—positive deck, good double-

70

down hands—and I lost them both. I was down $900 in three hands, and I didn't think things could get any worse. I was wrong! On the very next hand, Steven drew a pair of 7s against a dealer 7. He had bet $100 that hand, and added another $100 to split his pair. For his first hit he drew a 3, and another $100 slid into his circle to double-down. He asked for a hit on his second 7 and drew another 7. He added another $100 and split again. Again he asked for a hit on his second 7 and drew a 10. He stood, asked for a hit on his third 7—and drew another 7! Another split, and another $100. A hit on his third 7 drew an Ace and he stood. He asked for a hit on his last 7, and drew another 3! He doubled. Steven had started that hand with a $100 bet, and now he had $600 on the table! Now it was the dealer's turn. He turned up his hole card. Another 7. We were in total shock when the dealer's hit card turned out to be yet another 7! He had drawn a 21 and Steven lost all the way across. The dealer was apologizing as he took Steven's money. He said, "I'm sorry, I've been dealing a long time and have never seen anything like that." We lost $1,500 in four hands, and our heads were spinning. Steven said, "Jesus, I think I could use a drink." I looked at my watch. It was only 8:30 in the morning, but I agreed. It *was* time for a drink. We ended up losing $2,800 that trip.

Many of the books listed in the "References and Recommended Reading" section have discussions on risk, gambler's ruin, or other similarly depressing subjects. The most detailed discussion is in Bryce Carlson's book *Blackjack for Blood*. Mr. Carlson's discussion on the theory of gambler's ruin is comprehensive and filled with statistical analysis. Stanford Wong includes in his book *Professional Blackjack* a section entitled "Introduction to Win Rate and Risk." Ken Uston, in his book *Million Dollar Blackjack*, has a chapter entitled "Determination of Betting Strategy" that discusses negative swings, risk, and long-run expectations. These respected authors have some disagreement about the severity of the problem, but they agree that occasional losses will be an unfortunate fact of life for blackjack players. I highly recommend that you read them. You should pay particular attention to their discussions on total gambling stakes and trip stakes; both are necessary to provide some level of statistical protection to your gambling effort.

Playing a winning system provides you with an edge over the casino. However, I should say that this is a long-term advantage. Anything can happen in the short term, and the short term is where the problem lies. The fateful trip to Las Vegas which I mentioned earlier was a short-term problem. This is certainly not a common occurrence for me. If it were, I would take up Yahtzee instead of blackjack! However, since losing is a built-in part of winning, the question becomes: How much am I going to have to pay to play?

Properly determining how much money to take with you (your trip stake) is necessary to prevent you from going broke during a negative swing (short-term bad luck). You want to be able to keep playing even if you have had a day or two of losing. If you don't plan for this you might run out of money and have to spend all day watching ice hockey in the sports bar! Just the thought of that should motivate you to pay attention to your gambling stake! Steven and I each like to take around 120 table-minimum bets on every trip. Before each trip we decide on the casinos where we will be playing and the most likely amount of time we will be playing at $10 tables, $25 tables, and others. We then calculate our trip stake, go to the bank for travelers checks, and go.

We actually hedge a bit. If we lose half of our trip stake, then we automatically drop to the next lower table minimum. For example, if we made plans to play at $25 tables, we would each take $3,000 with us ($6,000 total). If we lose half of that, we then drop to the $10 tables. If we win back to our original stake, we move back to the $25 tables. This provides strong statistical protection to our stake, and to our peace of mind!

Negative swings are tough to deal with emotionally. Remember when you were playing the slots or roulette—or when you were playing blackjack before you learned how? You had hope, but it was without expectation. Now you have hope *with* expectation. There *is* a significant difference! Negative swings happen, so prepare yourself mentally.

As you save enough, or win enough, to start moving up to the higher-stakes games, your expected win rate will increase significantly. Remember the chart back in chapter 3, where I showed you the expected results at a $5 table with various levels of expertise? Let's look at it again, but this time using a $25 table with a $50 average bet for the typical and basic-system players, and a $62.50 average bet for the count-system player.

Expectation at Various Levels of Expertise
($25 Table)

	Typical "Jane" Player	Basic-System Player	Count-System Player
Casino Advantage	3.5%	0.5%	
Player Advantage			1.5%
Average Bet	$50.00	$50.00	$62.50
Action/Hour	$3,000.00	$3,000.00	$3,750.00
Loss/Hour	$105.00	$15.00	
Win/Hour			$56.25
Loss/Day (6 Hrs.)	$630.00	$90.00	
Win/Day (6 Hrs.)			$337.50
Three-Day Loss	$1,890.00	$270.00	
Three-Day Win			$1,012.50

Notice that your expected win has increased from $11.25 an hour at the $5 table to $56.25 an hour at the $25 table, and your trip expectation has increased from $202.50 to $1,012.50. Not bad, but it shows that you have to have money to make money. For a $100 table and a $250 average bet, this time you do the math. Your expectation is now $225 an hour! But remember, you stand to lose $10,000 or more during a bad negative swing at the $100 tables. Your expectation goes up, but so does your risk!

A strong word of caution is in order here. *Never, never, never* overplay your stake! We made that mistake several times early in our learning period, and it cost us every time. If you plan to play at a $10 table, then take around $1,200 for the trip, and don't let the $25 tables tempt you. Negative swings (short-term bad luck) can wipe you out! If you want to play $25 tables, take $3,000 with you, and don't let the $100 tables tempt you. Just be careful.

Now is a good time to mention your gambling fund again. You did establish one, didn't you? Your gambling fund is earmarked specifically for use in the casinos and contains no money otherwise critical to your life. Remember that when you encounter a negative swing; it will help when your emotions are running high. During a bad swing you may decide the system doesn't work, or that you're not good enough, or that the blackjack goddess simply hates you. Well, hang in there when nothing seems to be going right. The system works, you're good enough, and things will change. Remembering that the gambling fund is set up specifically for times like these will help. It does me.

If you are like I was and don't have enough money to fund the game at the statistically "safe" level, don't worry about it. If you can only come up with $200, go for it. If a negative swing wipes it out, well, so what. Save some more and go again. Your advantage will eventually show and you will win, but you have to play to win. Remember, unused skill gives you no advantage whatsoever over someone who has no skill.

Chapter Overview

Unfortunately, occasional losses are a built-in part of blackjack—even when you are playing a winning system. Recognizing and planning for the inevitable will help you emotionally, and controlling your emotions will make you a better player.

8

The Art

It's what you learn after you know it all that counts.

—UNKNOWN PHILOSOPHER

Is it enough? You now know how to play the game. You have studied and practiced, and the information, the charts, and the strategies are becoming second nature. The science (it's hidden behind the words) gives you the edge, but is it enough? Maybe, but there is also an art to winning.

Don't Do It

First, some basic don'ts.

Don't drink and play. Drinking slows you down and definitely makes you less diligent. The worst part is that you don't immediately recognize that you're slower and less alert. You don't have to be a complete teetotaler when you are playing, but be careful. I have determined that two alcoholic drinks are my limit. Beyond that I am no longer able to play, much less maintain the count. However, everyone is different; determine your tolerance for alcohol and don't over do it or it will cost you! You *can* act like you are drinking. The bosses like players who drink, because they generally lose a lot more money. Just order a Coke,

Sprite, or 7-Up. The pit boss is not going to check to see if there is rum or bourbon in it.

Don't play when you are tired. Being tired is similar to drinking; you are slower and less alert. How to judge when you are too tired is very subjective and will require some self-analysis. Sometimes I wake up tired and can play for only a couple of hours before I have to call it a day. At other times I can play for twelve hours and still feel alert. Always keep in mind that you are playing with a small percentage advantage, so don't give up that edge just because you are too stubborn to quit. Steven and I were particularly susceptible to the "last night stand." When we knew we had to go home the next day we were inclined to stay up late, sometimes all night. This type of play always cost us money. Don't do it.

Don't play if you have a bad attitude. Let's admit it, sometimes our moods will not allow us to play effective mind games with chauvinistic jerks. Cool it, then turn their attitude into chips.

Manage Your Money

You already know about the swings you can expect in your gambling fund. The only way to prevent swings is not to play, but that wouldn't be any fun, so let's look at some ways to reduce them. The first is to establish a loss limit for each casino session. Setting loss limits keeps you from going deeply in the hole with a hot dealer. I set a loss limit equal to my buy-in, and my buy-in is equal to twenty table-minimum bets. So if I'm playing at a $10 table my buy-in and loss limit is $200. If I lose my buy-in, I'm out of there. The hot-dealer phenomenon apparently has very little mathematical support, but few would deny it exists. There are times when you just cannot win under any conditions, so a loss limit will keep it under control. I don't always change my buy-in cash to chips at one time. I might sit down at a $10 table and buy $100 in chips, and then buy the other $100 in chips later if the need arises.

Quitting while you are winning is the next step in money management. I have often said, "If I had only quit when...." This statement was usually made after a session when I was considerably ahead and then lost most of my winnings. Not smart! I have since established a "quit a winner" rule. Now, anytime I get ahead by an amount equal to one-half of my buy-in, I will *not* leave that table a loser.

When I have gotten ahead by that amount, then my new loss limit becomes one-half of my *winnings*. If I was at that same $10 table and was $100 ahead (one-half of my $200 buy-in), then I establish a new loss limit of $50. This means that I will leave that table at least $50 ahead no matter what happens. It works for me.

Stash Your Winnings

If you are winning, the chance of attracting the attention of the bosses is greater. You want to win but you don't want attention, so putting a few chips in your purse or pocket now and then will reduce the attention a large and growing stack attracts. I stash a few every half-hour or so, usually when the dealer is looking the other way. Nothing's wrong with it; they are my chips to do with as I wish, but sometimes the dealer or pit boss might become curious. If one does catch me, I just say, "slot money." That's all they need and it is totally believable to them. After all, I'm just a woman. A very easy way to stash a few chips is when you are changing tables. When you get to the new table, just don't pull all your chips out of your purse or pocket to begin the new game.

Don't Be Cheated

Casino cheating is rare. In most places the casinos operate under state laws and regulations, and if they are caught cheating the players, they can be shut down. I just don't believe most would take that chance. However, at some of the small, struggling casinos they might be willing to take the chance just to increase their profits.

I have only been cheated once that I know of, and that was by a young "inexperienced" male dealer at just such a small, struggling casino. He didn't do it by smooth card handling, or by other methods that would have been impossible for me to detect. He would deal extremely fast, and would then get faster when it came time to complete his hand and collect the bets. In fact, he was so fast that he would deal his last card, announce his total, and pick up his cards before I could add his hand.

I was playing only basic strategy at the time, was fairly new to the game, and didn't immediately recognize that he was picking his cards up before he would collect mine (opposite from the way it is supposed to be done). Several times I thought I had won, but he had already picked his cards up and I was hesitant to say anything.

I finally couldn't stand it and said, "Hey, I think I beat you on that hand!" He was very nice and immediately spread his cards back out on the table. I *had* won, and he apologized profusely, saying he was a new dealer and how he appreciated my helping him keep track. It happened again, and he apologized and thanked me—again.

Such a nice lady, helping the new dealer grow in his job. It wasn't until later that I found out he wasn't new to the job. I am convinced that he cheated me because I was easy prey, a woman playing alone at his table. Steven informed me that this dealer had been there for some time. He also told me that the dealer hadn't gathered the cards out of order when he had played at his table. Oh, well—just be careful. If a good card handler wants to cheat you using card tricks, he will. You won't catch him, and if you did, you couldn't prove it. If you follow your rules—don't stay longer than one hour and hold to your loss limit— then even if you are cheated it won't ruin you. If you think you are being cheated, leave immediately.

Choosing a Table

Sometimes when you walk up to a table you will hear the other players moaning and groaning about how hot the dealer is. You will notice that there are very few chips stacked in front of the players. "He never busts, and he hasn't let us win in twenty minutes," they will tell you. Believe it and take your money to another table. Steven likes to have a mathematical explanation for everything, but he doesn't for hot dealers. He just says, "It happens."

Another clue to watch for is a dealer standing alone behind an empty blackjack table in a crowded casino. When I walk up to this table I will ask, "Doesn't anybody like you?" or "Did you run everybody off?" If I get an answer like, "I'm so hot that nobody lasts long," then I'm off to another table. The dealers will often be honest about their temperature. It happens.

There is a female dealer at the Santa Fe Casino in northern Las Vegas known as the Black Widow. A few years ago she was dealing at a $10 table when a man sat down and bought in for $100. Ten hands later his $100 was gone. He reached into his pocket for more money and said,

"You can't keep this up." Ninety hands and nine $100 bills later he said, "Lady, you are the Black Widow of blackjack." The pit boss verified that this story was true. He told me, "I have never seen a dealer as hot as our Black Widow!" It happens.

I once walked up to a dealer alone at a table and asked why he was alone. His reply was that everybody decided to go have breakfast. "Everybody decided to go have breakfast at once?" I asked. He just shrugged his shoulders. The pit boss was listening to our conversation and said, "If you believe that story, you'll believe anything!" We all laughed and I moved on.

Number of Players

When you are counting cards the number of players at the table becomes an important factor. If you are at a single-deck game with a full table of players, you can expect only two rounds of cards to be dealt between shuffles. This is not good. You don't have time to put your knowledge to work for you. A good rule of thumb is no more than two players per single deck, and no more than four players per double deck. You will find that it is difficult to follow this rule faithfully because players are constantly coming and going. You may sit down with two other players, and within minutes the table will fill. Given the option though, stay as close as possible to the rule. This is particularly critical at single-deck games. We have actually done pretty well at two-deck games with full tables, but the penetration, or depth, into a deck dealt *has* to be good. It is fine to play at full tables with more than two decks.

When to Play

If you are in a location where single- or double-deck games are available, stay away from the higher-deck games. Remember, the more decks there are, the higher the casino advantage. However, playing at a single-deck game with a full table is worse than playing at a six-deck game. Therefore, finding casinos which have good rules and few players at the tables is important. If you have the option of playing during the week, you will find the playing conditions a little better than on a weekend. The casinos will not have as many tables open for play, but it is still better. Playing early in the morning, after 4 A.M., is good. If we play on a weekend, we will often go to bed early, and then get up early. (If you do this, it is important not to look like you just showered and put on fresh clothes—look more like you've been up all night). Another good time to play is late in the afternoon, between 4 P.M. and 6 P.M. I'm not sure what everyone is doing, but it seems that there is a lull in the action at that time.

Where to Sit

Counting cards eventually gets so easy that you can do it with just a glance at the cards as they are turned up. However, if you sat at the middle of the table you would have to turn your head both ways to glance at the cards, like watching a tennis match. It could start to look suspicious, so just sit close to either end. I prefer to sit one place from either end. The player on "first base," on the dealer's far left, is the first to play and therefore noticed more. The player on "third base," on the dealer's far right, is the last to play and usually noticed *much* more. The other players will often hold the third-base player responsible for how the dealer does. You will sometimes hear someone tell a third-base player, "If you hadn't taken that ten, the dealer would have busted and all of us would have won!"

Realistically, how anyone plays their hand has very little to do with the others' outcome, but some people believe it does, so don't sit at third base if you are counting. If you are not counting but have a partner who is, you can sit anywhere. You don't even have to sit next to your partner, and you don't even have to indicate that you are acquainted.

Tipping

When I first started playing, I thought that tipping dealers was on the same level as tipping the waiter or waitress. I wasn't sure of how much to tip, but I sure didn't want to offend the dealer, so I tipped too much, *way* too much. In my observation, women are the biggest tippers at the blackjack tables. Beware, you are tipping away your winnings, and the dealers love it. Tipping the dealers is totally at the player's discretion, so use it to your benefit. There are times when tipping will put the dealer on your side, particularly when the dealer knows that you tip only out of your winnings.

How can the dealer help you? The most obvious is after a dealer peeks at his hole card to see if he has a blackjack. Sometimes, being the "don't know how to play very well woman" that I am, I will innocently ask the dealer what I should do with my hand. Occasionally the dealer, who knows what the hole card is and also that I tip when I win, will tell me how to play my hand. "I can't tell you what to do, but if it were me, I wouldn't hit it," might be the response. Interpretation: *I have a low card in the hole, and I'm likely to bust, so don't hit your 15.*

A dealer may also help by simply "playing" my hand. This has happened to me several times, where I simply showed the dealer my cards with the most confused look I could muster, and the dealer did the rest. In these situations, he may immediately pass me by and go on to the next player, or he may give me a hit. I always tip after receiving this type of "assistance."

How deeply the dealer penetrates into the deck before shuffling is extremely important to the card-counter. Tipping when the dealer is trying to decide whether or not to deal one more hand will occasionally help them wait to shuffle. I always try this at least once, to test the dealer when the count is at +SIPS.

There are two ways to tip. One is to just give the dealer the tip, and the other is to place a bet for him or her. Most dealers prefer you to place their bet, but I generally ask the dealer which they would prefer. Again, it's easy to get carried away and end up giving a good part of your winnings to the dealer. Use good judgment. If I'm not winning, I'm not tipping.

Zero Count, Zero Bet

If you are sitting at the table, you are expected to bet and play. This is a disgusting thing for them to expect when the count is at 0 or below and the casino has the advantage! Of course, they don't know what the count is, and they don't know that *you* know. So some money-saving techniques are in order. Sometimes I will "forget" to bet, mostly because I am so involved in a conversation that I just forget what I am supposed to do! At other times I will pout because I lost the last hand and just refuse to bet. The dealer will let you get by with this as long as you don't do it too often. Also, it seems inevitable that I have to go to the lady's room when the count reaches −SIPS. It just happens—must be all that coffee. Another option is to just ask the dealer to shuffle, especially if everyone at the table has been losing. Sometimes they'll do it! You won't know until you ask.

Don't Tell Them You Count

Casino personnel are constantly on the lookout for card-counters. They pay attention mostly to men, but don't assume that they aren't watching you. There are several things that a floorman or pit boss will watch for that you should avoid. One is your bet spread. I told you earlier how I do mine, but I am careful. If the pit boss happens to be standing at my table and visiting with the dealer, I may be even a little more conservative in raising or lowering my bets.

Intensity is something casino personnel pay close attention to. Counting cards while you act like you are ignoring them, making decisions while you visit with your neighbor, and generally seeming like a "typical female" is difficult. It can be done, but you will have to work at it while you act like you aren't working at anything. Don't let this scare you because it actually becomes much easier with practice.

Another thing you need to be particularly careful of is watching the floorman or pit boss yourself. If they think you are concerned about what they are doing, they are likely to get concerned about what you are doing. Be aware of them, but don't watch them.

The big-bet shuffle is another potential problem. This can happen when the count has reached + SIPS and you have placed your maximum bet before the dealer decides to shuffle. If you were careful, you might have waited to make your bet to see if he was going to deal one more round before the shuffle, but it doesn't always happen that way. When that happens to me, I pull my bet out of the circle and act very indecisive about what to bet. I may ask the dealer if he can remember if I won the first hand of the last deck. No matter what he responds, I will decide to make only a small bet because "I never win two first-dealt hands," or "If I lost the last one, then I sure don't want to bet big on this one." Pulling back a big bet during a shuffle is something the bosses watch for, so be careful. Occasionally, particularly if the pit boss is close, I will leave my big bet out.

The last thing to be careful of is lousy hand insurance. You have learned to insure at + SIPS. But what does it look like when the dealer has an Ace up and you chose to insure a 14? The other players will remark about your decision and the dealer might say, "That was a pretty lousy hand to insure." And the pit boss may wonder what's going on. Remember that the count is high and so is your bet. You need to insure, so be ready! I always say, "Well, he had a blackjack the last two times," or "He didn't have one the last time, so I thought he might this time." Say anything to lead them to believe that it was just good intuition by a very lucky lady.

How Often Per Casino

Steven and I are careful about how often we show our faces in each casino. If we play at the same place too often, we may be recognized and be under more scrutiny than we want. We have a rule for this: no more than one session per shift, per casino, per month. There are currently forty-five casinos in Las Vegas that have good rules (each with three shifts per day), so even with our rule there is no shortage of places to play. We can safely play for 135 hours per month, six hours per day, which means 22.5 days of play every month. That's a lot. With this much opportunity available, there is just no reason to overexpose ourselves at any casino. *Keeping good records is an absolute requirement* for this. We record the casino, the date, and the time immediately after each session.

Like all rules, these call for exceptions. Sometimes we play on Indian reservations or in towns with few casinos where following the one session per shift, per casino, per month rule is not practical. In these situations we just do the best we can. We will play more conservatively than normal and may even spend a few minutes playing Triple Action or Double Exposure. Doing this will "prove" to any curious pit bosses that we don't know what we are doing.

Don't Feel Like You Are Cheating

Several of my close friends, who know that I count cards, have asked if counting is cheating or illegal. Of course, the answer is no. It's not cheating, and it's not illegal. You are neither using a mechanical or electronic device nor are you marking cards or using any other cheating method. You are simply using your brain.

However, when you first learn to play effective blackjack, you may feel uneasy in the casinos. While you know that you are not doing anything wrong, you may feel like you are. Experience will quickly get you over this feeling, but at first you may feel guilty. I did. I was even embarrassed when I won!

Well, if it helps, always remember that the casinos have designed their games for the sole purpose of taking your money! They don't feel guilty, so why should you?

So What If You Get Caught

I can say "so what" in a very casual way because in all the years I've played blackjack I have never been caught and kicked out of a casino. However, I am a card-counter and it may happen one day. At first I was horrified at the thought, but I have now accepted the fact that it could happen, and if it does I will simply walk calmly out of the casino and have my nervous breakdown on the sidewalk. Actually, I do have a plan, and just having it helps my attitude. You have to accept the possibility, however remote it may be, that it could happen to you. Think about it. If it happens, it really isn't the end of the world. I believe the best thing to do is just leave. Don't fuss about it, just leave. After all, there are lots of casinos with lots of chandeliers.

I personally believe that kicking out good blackjack players is contrary to the rules of fair play. They invite us to play, but they don't want us to know how. It's kind of like inviting us to enter a cooking contest but not letting us participate if we know how to cook.

The Partners Game

I just can't say enough about playing partners. This method of ganging up on the casino is great. I've already told you about many of the advantages, so let me spend a few minutes telling you about some of the acts it will let you play. I'll give you one example entitled "The Rivalry."

A husband and wife sit down at a $25 table and complete the initial hellos to the dealer. The husband then says, "How much you wanna bet this time?" The wife responds, "Nothing, you beat me the last two times." "Oh, how about just a small bet, say the loser buys dinner?" Then the wife says to the dealer, "Will you help me beat this jerk? I'm already behind by two show tickets, and his head is getting too big." The dealer is only slightly interested, but is getting the idea that beating the casino is not the goal of these players.

She goes on, "I'll tell you what. You help me beat him and I'll share my winnings with you." The wife buys in for $300 and the husband for $200. The pit boss comes by and the dealer tells him, "We've got a small tournament going on between these two." The pit boss smiles. The underdog normally gets the sympathy, so as the game proceeds the wife is wildly raising and lowering her bets, trying to beat her husband, and the dealer is secretly pulling for her. In fact, the dealer has completely forgotten to announce "checks play" to the pit boss.

The husband makes comments like "I've got you now," when she makes larger bets than he does. The pit boss loves it because the couple only cares about beating each other. Occasionally, the boss stops by to wish the lady luck. The dealer helps her when he can, and the husband will say, "Hey, us guys are supposed to stick together." The session ends in about an hour with the wife finally "beating" her husband, but he's a good sport and predicts it won't happen again. The dealer is happy because she was tipping, and the pit boss was amused. For some reason, the husband and wife were both smiling on their way to the cashier.

This example is just one among many that partners can use to direct attention away from their skillful play. You will find that your imagination will come up with an endless list. Think about it; how about "The Grouchy Husband," or "The First Time I Ever Played This Game," or "The Defiant Woman Who Is Playing With Her Money and Will Bet It However She Wants To," or…as I said, the list is endless. If you choose to act, then be sure it seems natural and can be done convincingly.

Chapter Overview

The following A and S (Angie and Steven) Rules include not only what is in this chapter, but also all the essential, vital, and indispensable potpourri scattered throughout the book. Our rules were established after a lot of experience and many mistakes, so look them over and adopt them. You will eventually establish your own set of rules, but for now stick to ours.

A and S Rules

1. Know your stuff.
2. Do not drink and play.
3. Do not play while tired.
4. If possible, play only at one- or two-deck games with average to good penetration.
5. Play one-deck games with a maximum of two players.
6. It is desirable to have no more than four players at a two-deck game, but it is okay to play at a full table if the penetration is good.
7. Play only at games with a 0.5 percent or less casino advantage (calculated for basic play). A 0.3 percent or less casino advantage is much more desirable.
8. Play a flexible one-hour session, a maximum of one per shift, per casino, per month.
9. Keep accurate records.
10. Do not overplay your stake.
11. Take 120 table-minimum bets for the trip stake.
12. If a negative swing reduces the trip stake by half, drop to the next lower table minimum, i.e., $25 to $10, or $10 to $5.
13. Establish a buy-in and session-loss limit of twenty times the table minimum.
14. If you're ahead by one-half of the buy-in amount, establish a new loss limit of one-half of the amount ahead.
15. Sit one seat from either end of the table if at all possible.
16. Dress according to location, average bet size, and any special events. *Do not stand out!*

9

Let's Dress Up/Down

That the birds of worry and care fly over your head,
this you cannot change, but that they build nests in
your hair, this you can prevent.

—CHINESE PROVERB

"Pack your bags, we're leaving for Las Vegas tonight," said Steven over
the phone. This was a surprise! Special-rate flight tickets were available
and he couldn't pass them up. I quickly placed the receiver on the
phone and dashed to the hamper. I hadn't done laundry all week!

My luggage was laying on our bed, and I was staring blankly into the
closet. Our trips to Las Vegas were running together in my head. I just
couldn't remember what casinos we had concentrated on last trip. I
quickly located our trip notes from a month earlier, and found Arizona
Charlie's, the Santa Fe, Sam's Town, and the downtown casinos listed.
Good! This time we would be spending our time on the Strip. I loved
our Strip trips. We would be playing higher-stakes games, and the
lights, glitter, fountains, and overall atmosphere was just more exciting
to me. And I could take my dressier clothes and good jewelry.

You may be wondering what difference it makes. Well, your trip
wardrobe is extremely important. Playing effective blackjack requires

87

that you go unnoticed by the casino bosses. Oh, they may notice you, but—well, you know what I mean. What you don't want is attention because you look out of place. On our last trip I dressed in pants, flats, and sweaters. Steven wore jeans and tennis shoes. The casinos we were playing in attracted locals, and the more casual tourist crowd. We had to "fit in" and be as invisible as possible.

On this trip, we would be playing in casinos frequented by the more ritzy crowd. I knew that at some point we would be sitting at a $100 table at the Mirage. I would have on a dress, heels, and jewelry. The pit boss would be able to tell that I could afford to play, and lose, at high-stakes games. I will, of course, have absolutely no intention of losing, and dressing the part will simply allow me to do my thing. I will be "invisible."

Special occasions are sometimes a major factor in choosing your trip wardrobe. In Las Vegas, one of these occasions is the National Finals Rodeo. This is a weeklong event held in early December of each year. Boots, jeans, hats, western shirts, and western dresses are the most common attire you will find in every casino. I love western clothes, so this is one of my favorite trips each year.

Weather and walking are two other prime considerations in choosing what clothes to take. It may be comfortable in the casinos, but outside it may be freezing, or sizzling hot. Wherever you are going, be prepared for the prevalent temperature. It may be a lot different than back home! I have a pretty narrow temperature tolerance and actually get cool in the casinos, so I usually carry a light jacket or sweater with me, even in the summer.

Your choice of shoes is of critical importance. You will be doing a lot of walking, and you know how bad that can be if your feet hurt! Be sure the shoes you take are comfortable. On those occasions when you are wearing heels, be sure to drive or take a taxi between casinos.

If Las Vegas is where you do most of your gambling, then I highly recommend that you subscribe to the *Las Vegas Advisor*, a helpful monthly newsletter that provides all sorts of information about Las Vegas. Some examples are: dining, entertainment, and a three-month advance planner, which includes important dates, tournaments, and the weather. This newsletter has helped us a lot, and I know you will thoroughly enjoy it. Their address is listed in our "References and Recommended Reading."

If you are planning a trip other than to Las Vegas, I would suggest that you contact the local chamber of commerce. They will gladly provide you information on happenings during the dates you plan to visit. In addition, watch the weather forecast for at least a week before your trip. This will give you some idea of the appropriate clothing to take.

The last thing to remember is to be comfortable with whatever you have decided to wear. And don't let the birds nest in your hair—this might draw more attention than you want!

Chapter Overview

How you dress is a very important part of playing successful blackjack. In planning your trip wardrobe, always consider the most probable type of crowd that will be present in the casinos you plan to visit, your average bet size, special events, weather, and comfort. Just *don't* stand out!

10

Let's Eat for Free

There is a time to let things happen and a time to
make things happen.

—HUGH PRATHER

I was laughing so hard my eyes were watering. "What's the matter, don't
you like your steak?"

"No...yes, it's good, but you shouldn't have done that."

"I shouldn't have done what?"

"You wouldn't have done it if you had known I was listening, would
you?"

"Probably not, now quit laughing and eat your dinner."

Steven grew up close to the west Texas border and must have had
quite a drawl when he left there to go to college. It doesn't show much
now, but he can slip back into the accent, including an exaggerated
dialect, and be a real country bumpkin anytime he wants to—and I
guess he wanted to that evening. We were playing at a casino on the
Strip and I was ahead. I was also getting hungry, so I told Steven I was
ready for a dinner break. He glanced at my chips and said, "Okay, but
why don't you hit the slots for a few minutes, and then I'll find you and
we'll eat." I stopped at a machine behind the tables and was thinking,
he's up to something.

It happened just a few minutes later, and I was listening. The pit boss was approaching the table and Steven got up from his seat and said, "Sir, have ya got jist a minute, cause I bin want'n to ask ya sumthin'?" The pit boss was nice, "Sure, how can I help you?" Steven started, "Well, back home a lotta ma friends tell how they stay for free, and eat for free when they come over here, and I ain't never got nothin'. When I told 'em that, they told me that ya gotta ask for it, an then one of 'em even told me that with as much money as I drop over here they otta buy me a condo just to keep me here. I thought that took a lotta balls, but anyway, I'm kinda embarrassed to ask, but I would like to tell those boys that I got to eat for nothin'. So I was jist wonderin' if ya might have some spare supper tickets that you haven't used. Ya know, just so I can tell 'em." Steven looked serious, and the pit boss was grinning, almost laughing, "How many do you need?"

Steven went on, "Well, my wife's around here somewhere. You know, she won a little at blackjack last night and then she lost it all in a slot machine—but ya watch, when she gets back home she's gonna tell 'em how she won. Don't them women beat all. They do have some redeemin' qualities though, don'cha think? Anyway, I guess I could use a couple of 'em." The pit boss comped him the free meals and Steven said, "Thanks, now I owe ya one, so if ya ever get over to Muleshoe ya be sure to look me up!"

The pit boss just wanted to get away from this turnip seed, and I wasn't sure I wanted to be seen with him myself. But we were eating for free and that's what this chapter is all about.

Comps are an integral part of the casino atmosphere. They are given to players to keep them at that casino—actually, to keep them losing money at that casino. Free stuff comes in every imaginable form, but the most common are drinks, meals, shows, and rooms. High-stakes players (or *whales,* as they are sometimes called), also receive free travel expenses.

We prefer not to take advantage of comps, or at least not very often. Comps are based on the average bet size and the time played. To get them we would generally have to be rated by the pit boss, and this causes us to receive a little more attention than we would like. Also, it normally requires us to play longer at any given casino than we like, however, there are exceptions. If we have been playing at a $25 table for at least an hour, we will occasionally ask if we have played long enough to qualify for a comp. More often than not, particularly if we are playing together, we qualify for a free trip to the buffet or coffee shop. Buffets are not bad, and coffee shops are good. Coffee shops serve everything from sandwiches to steaks, and sometimes they will include crab or lobster on the menu. In many of the downtown casinos, playing at $10 tables for an hour will qualify for coffee shop meals.

I guess we have been going to casinos long enough to be on everyone's mailing list. We are constantly receiving promotional advertisements for free rooms, or reduced-priced rooms, and we definitely take advantage of these. Free meals are often included with the promotions. We will get a flurry of these right before the Thanksgiving and Christmas holidays. December is a fairly slow month for the casinos, so it is a good month to look for deals.

We actually encourage the casinos to keep us informed by joining their slot clubs, because members are often offered deals not available to the average blackjack player. This doesn't mean that we play the slots much, but we try to put our cards in the machines often enough to keep our memberships active.

I have already mentioned the *Las Vegas Advisor*. We also use it to keep us informed of the best buys on rooms, meals, and entertainment. This monthly newsletter is very good. Again, I highly recommend it to anyone who goes to Las Vegas more than once a year. It includes a number of coupons with a subscription (for free meals, rooms, and others perks) which more than pays for the cost of the publication. I also recommend that you purchase a copy of *Bargain City*. Anthony Curtis, who is the publisher of the *Las Vegas Advisor*, wrote this book. It is packed with great information on saving money in Las Vegas.

Chapter Overview

Keeping trip expenses down simply adds to your winnings, so take advantage of free stuff and discounts when you can. However, getting discounts along with the risk of being caught as a skilled blackjack player is not a good tradeoff.

11

Blackjack Tournaments

The will to win is not nearly as important as the will
to prepare to win.

—BOBBY KNIGHT

"Well, he beat me," Steven resolved. I snapped, "No he didn't, you let him win!" My comment reflected my observation of how Steven had bet on the last hand. It was Steven's first tournament, and he was playing his normal game. He had done well and was $50 ahead of his closest competitor going into the last hand of the game. The count must have been good, because Steven placed a $100 bet. I was excited until I noticed that his competitor had placed a $200 bet. With a good count I knew that they might both win their hands. I wanted to tell Steven to bet more, but I couldn't and he didn't. He won the hand and lost the tournament. I later apologized for snapping at him, but as an observer, I had noticed what Steven had not.

A few weeks later you would have thought that Steven had discovered the secret to the universe. He was excited when he showed me the outcome chart and playing strategy he had been working on, and said, "You were right, I should have bet more. Tournament play is sure a lot different than regular blackjack." His chart made a lot of sense, and I was pretty proud of myself for steering him in the right direction.

His ego was later deflated when he discovered that he was not the only one, nor was he even the first, to have discovered this secret. Stanford Wong also had. Steven had ordered a copy of his book *Casino Tournament Strategy,* and we were very impressed with his section on blackjack. While his strategy is somewhat different than ours, it is based on the same premise. I highly recommend that you read it. Mr. Wong has also developed a software program called Tournament Blackjack. Our computer is just not new enough or big enough to run the program so we haven't purchased it, but you can bet that if it has his name on it, it's accurate and understandable. If you're interested, you can contact him at the Pi Yee Press. The address is listed in "References and Recommended Reading."

We now have considerable experience playing in blackjack tournaments, and Steven believes that tournaments are half luck, half talent, and half witchcraft. I think he is half right. Well, anyway, I think that tournament play is half talent and half luck. This chapter explains the talent part. Kissing up to the blackjack goddess is up to you.

Fun and Serious

Blackjack tournaments are starting to show up everywhere. They are exciting, fun, and can be profitable. However, if you intend to play in tournaments, there are some things you need to learn—*and* some things you need to unlearn.

Blackjack tournaments come in every size and shape, but they break into two major categories, which we call fun and serious. In the fun tournaments the entrance fee is between $20 and $100, and no buy-in is required. The casino provides each player with $500 worth of nonnegotiable tokens at the beginning of each round. Prize money is between $500 and $1,000 for first place, and between $200 and $400 for second place. Much smaller prizes are generally offered to all the players who make it to the final round. Fun tournaments are normally held at casinos on a regularly scheduled basis. For example, one may hold tournaments every Monday and Wednesday morning at 9 A.M., while another may hold one every Thursday night at 6 P.M. We have also discovered that most of the fun tournaments are not well advertised, so you may have to spend some time locating them, either on the phone, or by asking during your regular casino play.

In the serious tournaments the entrance fee ranges from $200 to $500 or more, and you are required to buy in, generally at $500, at the beginning of each round. Sometimes you are required to pay your buy-in amount at the cashier and take a receipt to the table to receive your tournament chips. The prize money offered at these tournaments is substantial. While it is different at every tournament, first place is sometimes rewarded with $100,000; second place may get around $30,000; and even the seventh place winner may receive $5,000. In these tournaments any chips you have at the end of each round are yours, just as in regular blackjack. If you decide to become involved in serious tournaments, ask all the major casinos to place you on their tournament information mailing list.

I recommend that you play in a few fun tournaments before moving on to the more serious events. This will give you a chance to get used to the tournament atmosphere and rules before you invest more money in the game.

Tournament Rules

While there are considerable differences in entrance fees, buy-in amounts, and prize money between fun tournaments and serious tournaments, most of the other rules are similar. I have listed these below, but please remember to always read a copy of the specific rules of the tournament you are entering.

1. A set number of hands, usually twenty to sixty, are dealt to each player during a round.

2. If you run out of chips you are not allowed to buy in again. If you go broke, you are out of the game.

3. You will play each seat of the table in a rotating manner, but you won't have to play musical chairs. This is accomplished by placing a marker in front of the first-base player, then moving it one place to the dealer's right before every deal. The player with the marker is the new first base, and is therefore the first to bet and the first to play. The dealer will require that the first-base player bet first, and then will work clockwise, requiring each player to place their bet if they have not already done so. In some tournaments the first-base player for the first hand is chosen by a roll of the dice.

4. Your chips must remain exposed and arranged neatly by color at

all times. You are not allowed to hide black chips under your red ones!
Actually you will find that tournament chips are often different colors
than normal casino chips. Pink may be worth $25; white may be worth
$100; and so forth. Pay attention to this!

5. Betting minimums and maximums are established for each
tournament. The minimum is generally $5 or $10, and the maximum
will range from $200 to $500. You are sometimes required to make your
bets in multiples of $10, i.e., you can bet $10 or $20, but you can't bet
$15 or $25. In tournament play the minimum means just that, the
absolute minimum. You are no longer allowed to sit out a hand when the
count gets to −SIPS, so, be sure to hit the powder room before the
tournament starts. Also, most tournaments will not let you change a bet
once you make it, so be sure you have it right to begin with.

6. The number of players at each table who will advance to the next
round varies at individual tournaments. (See why you have to check
individual tournament rules?) Generally, though, you will find that the
top two money winners from each table will advance to round two, but
then only the top winner from each table will advance to round three
(the semifinals), and the same goes for advancing from round three to
round four (the finals). Many of the serious tournaments will have four
hundred or more entrants, so it takes four rounds to narrow them down
to only one table. Some of the fun tournaments limit the number of
entrants, so only two or three rounds may be required to determine the
winners.

7. Most tournaments, but not all, will allow you to play in round two
even if you did not advance by virtue of being the first- or second-place
money winner at a table during round one. This is accomplished by
charging a reentry fee. At the fun tournaments it is generally equal to
the original entry fee, $20 to $100. At the serious tournaments it is
around one-third of the original fee. So if you originally paid $500,
expect to be out $165 to reenter.

Attitude

In regular blackjack your goal is, of course, to beat the casino, and you
could generally care less how the other players are doing. In
tournament play your goal is to beat the other players, no matter how
you are doing against the casino. This type of play takes a great deal of

mental adjustment, or at least it did for me. All the things we have learned about loss limits, bet spreads, pit boss scrutiny, and rigid count-based play no longer apply; in fact, they are sometimes completely contradictory to good tournament strategy.

Attitude, is what Steven calls it. He says the old "kill or be killed," or "win at any cost" attitude must be inserted into your mind if you are to stand a chance at tournament blackjack. To my mind this is a little harsh, but the reality is that you have to be willing to either win or lose it all trying.

This attitude is easy to adopt at the fun tournaments, where all you will lose is the original entry fee. However, maintaining this attitude during a serious tournament can be difficult. Picture this: you are in a serious tournament and have been incredibly lucky during the first fifty hands of the second round. You have turned the original $500 buy-in into $1,800. You have been betting big and the cards have been very cooperative. However, you weren't betting as big, nor were you as lucky as another lady. She has $2,400 in front of her. You are the only one at the table within striking distance of her, and she is not going to make it easy. She had been betting $200 to $300 a hand, but now she has $10 in her betting circle. "Oh damn," you will say (I guarantee it). Here are your options: 1. you can bet small and be almost assured of leaving the table and tournament with $1,800 in your purse; or, 2. you can go for it knowing that you only have a small chance of catching her and a large chance of losing a big portion of your $1,800. I know how difficult it is, but always remember that your only purpose in entering the tournament is to win the $100,000 first prize, and you *have* to be willing to lose it all in your pursuit of that goal. This attitude alone will put you ahead of more than half of the other competitors. When you combine attitude with good tournament strategy, you will then become a serious contender in any tournament.

Tournament Strategy

Steven and I have concluded that there are two important segments to every tournament round: the first half, and (you guessed it) the second half. The strategies for these two segments are so different that I treat them almost like two completely separate games.

During the first half of a round (the first thirty hands of a sixty-hand round) it is important to play as good a game as you can, and you should basically ignore the other players at the table. If you count, then base your betting and playing on the count. If you are playing basic strategy, then play your normal game. In either case, though, you should be slightly more aggressive with your betting than you normally would. Since there is no pit boss scrutiny during a tournament, you can raise and lower your bets as you desire. In my case, I count the cards, play the count strategy, and bet $5 (if that is the table minimum) when the count is minus, $25 if it is plus, and $50 if it has reached +SIPS. If I were playing basic strategy, I would bet $20 on each hand. You will notice that some of the players will be betting very large amounts, sometimes $200 or $300 per hand. Don't worry about them at this point. You have seen this before—they are more likely to go broke than get significantly ahead. Concentrate on *your* hands, and play them as well as you can.

Now comes the second half. During this segment, the blackjack goddess is going to play a big role, so be nice to her! It is now time to count your money and the other players' to determine your position. Remember, you are only interested in first place. You will either be ahead, behind, or tied. If you are ahead, you will want to protect and increase your lead. If you are behind, you want to catch up. If you are tied, it simply means that you are not ahead, and you will want to establish a lead and increase it.

At this point in the game, you need to drastically change the way you are playing. If you have been counting cards, then stop and start playing basic strategy. You are going to be very busy keeping track of the other players money and calculating your own bets. At this point it is absolutely necessary to understand the importance of adding up the money value of chips. Losing the tournament by $5 is the same as losing by $5,000. Don't let this happen to you just because you failed to accurately count your opponent's money.

You will notice that the chips, although stacked neatly by color, will vary significantly in type between the players. One player may have a small stack of $100 chips, a huge stack of $25 chips, and a moderate stack of $5 chips. Another may have mostly $100 chips and only a few $5 chips. When you are adding up their monetary value, it's just not good enough to say, "Well the guy on the end has four or five black ones, around twenty green ones, and maybe ten or fifteen red ones, so he has between a thousand and twelve hundred dollars." You need to practice adding chip values at home, so find some chips of the same size as casino chips and plan for several hours to get good enough for tournament play. If you have trouble finding chips of the right size (plastic poker chips are too small), you can try the Gamblers General Store, or the Bud Jones Company, both in Las Vegas. Their addresses are included in "References and Recommended Reading."

When I mentioned the blackjack goddess and her importance at this stage of the game, I was serious. Luck will now play a much bigger role than you are used to in normal blackjack. However, knowing a little more about the game will give you an edge over the other players. You can have good luck and fall further behind, or you can have bad luck and still make significant gains on your opponents. How can this be? Remember, at this point you are still playing against the dealer, but your emphasis, concentration, and strategy has to be on the other players, particularly the one in first place or the one who is threatening you if you are in first place. So if you bet $50 and win the hand, that's good, right? Not necessarily. Your opponent may have bet $100 and won. Even though you won, you fell further behind. You may have lost that same $50 bet, but if your opponent lost more, then you gained. Whether or not you beat the dealer has now faded in importance compared to how you are doing against the other player. When you are competing against another player, there are nine possible outcomes to every hand:

1. You both win.
2. You both lose.
3. You win, he loses.
4. You lose, he wins.
5. You push, he loses.
6. You push, he wins.
7. You win, he pushes.
8. You lose, he pushes.
9. You both push.

To play effective strategy you have to recognize the importance of these possible outcomes, however, calculating the results for all of them can get terribly confusing, so let's shorten it. Pushes are a pesky thing in the latter part of a blackjack tournament game, but they play a small role in tournament strategy. We can eliminate them with only small pulls on

our conscience. Don't worry, we'll get back to them, but for now you
have only four outcomes to consider:

1. You both win.
2. You both lose.
3. You win, he loses.
4. You lose, he wins.

Now we're getting somewhere. Whatever your position in relation to
the other players, these four outcomes become paramount in
importance. Depending on the blackjack goddess is fine, but playing a
strategy with better odds will help you—just in case she is having a bad
hair day.

In the latter part of a tournament round, betting, when combined
with the four outcomes listed above, becomes your only real weapon.
Remember, normally you will be concentrating on one other player, so
when compared to that player you can only bet more than, the same as,
or less than he does. What you should do depends on your position, so
let's combine the three betting possibilities with the four possible
outcomes and see if we can start making some sense out of this
discussion. The following table will show the results. Your betting, as
compared to another player, is shown across the top. You will either bet
more, the same, or less than he does. The four possible outcomes are
listed along the left side of the chart and the results are listed in the
body. You will either lose ground, remain the same, or gain ground.

Outcome/Betting Results

	Bet More	Bet the Same	Bet Less
You both win.	Gain	Same	Lose
You both lose.	Lose	Same	Gain
You win, he loses.	Gain	Gain	Gain
You lose, he wins.	Lose	Lose	Lose

Now, let's put those results to practical use. Suppose you are ahead in
the tournament. Should you bet less, the same, or more than your
opponent? If you are ahead, your primary effort will be to protect your
lead—you certainly don't want to lose ground! Look at the chart. If you

bet more than your opponent, or less, you would expect to lose on half of the outcomes and gain on the other half. But if you bet the same, you would lose ground on only one of the outcomes and maintain, or increase, your lead on the other three. This is by far the best option, since protecting your lead is your priority.

Suppose you are behind. Should you bet more, the same, or less than your opponent? Again, look at the chart. When you are in this position, your entire effort has to be in gaining. Contrary to the previous example, maintaining your position is not acceptable. So you should either bet more than your opponent, or less. You will gain with half of the outcomes. If you bet the same, you would gain on only one of the outcomes. However, in your effort to catch up, you are also exposing yourself to more chances to lose ground. Remember, attitude.

In a real tournament game, you will rarely find competitors who are familiar with outcomes and the power of betting. Most tournament players will fall into one of three general types. The first I call "Wimpy Wanda." Wimpy Wanda will bet small for the entire game and hope that everyone else goes broke. The second is "Aggressive Arnold." Aggressive Arnold will bet big for most of the game, even if he is ahead. The third type is "Erratic Ed." Erratic Ed is always looking nervously around the table and will be totally unpredictable in his betting. He just doesn't have a plan, not even a bad one. Steven and I have both concluded that Aggressive Arnold poses the biggest threat. He will more often than not be the type of player you are competing against. This observation has led us to a general strategy that we apply in those situations where being wimpy or aggressive seem to be of equal value. In these cases we always choose the aggressive option.

Back to the chart. I am going to combine the betting "more than" and "less than" columns and call it simply "more or less." So, the "more or less" strategy means that if your opponent bets large you bet less, or if your opponent bets small, you bet more. This method of betting will always be an important weapon when you are trying to catch up.

How much more or less you should bet when using this strategy depends on how far behind you are. If you are behind by $50 and your opponent has bet $200, you might want to bet $150. If you both lose the hand, then you are tied for the lead. If you both win, then you are only $100 behind and can adjust your bet on the next hand.

Up until now you have learned four very important aspects of tournament strategy. They are: (1) attitude, (2) betting more or less when behind, (3) betting the same when ahead, and (4) being aggressive. These strategies alone will make you a better tournament player. Now let's consider those situations when these strategies simply don't seem to apply. You need some additional options. After all, there are exceptions to every rule.

Sometimes you will find yourself in a situation where you are considerably behind and first place is actually shared by two players. They may not have exactly the same amount of money, but from your perspective they are equal. You need to catch both of them, and you know you should be betting more or less, but they won't let you. One of them is always betting the table maximum while the other is always betting the minimum. What should you do? If you are in the closing hands of the game, with ten or less hands remaining, you have no choice. Bet the maximum you can and stay with it until you get ahead, go broke, or the game ends. On the other hand, if there are twenty or more hands left in the game you can try a different approach. I'm sure there are hundreds of variations on this, but I have named the one I use "long shot." When I am in my long-shot mode, I ignore the other two players, at least for a short period of time, and concentrate only on my hands and my money. My goal is to significantly increase my money, but I want to be able to maintain my effort. In other words, I don't want to go broke too quick; after all, there are still twenty hands left. So I bet half my money or the table maximum, whichever is less.

Let's say that the table maximum is $300 and I have $400. The top two players have $1,100 (ugh!). I would bet $200. If I win I would have $600. I would then bet $300. If I win that hand I would have $900 and would again bet the maximum, $300. If I win that one, I would have $1,200, and I would be back in the game. If that happened I would also promise not to say another bad thing about the blackjack goddess! It can happen, but more than likely you are going to lose some hands. Betting half your money or the table maximum, whichever is less, will simply keep you in the game longer. This will provide you with more time to take advantage of a string of wins. Three or four straight wins can often put you back in a game. It can happen, so don't give up when you get behind!

You can (almost) find yourself in the same situation when you are ahead. Your two nearest competitors may have approximately the same amount of money, and they may be betting opposite of each other. This prohibits you from betting the same to protect your lead. What should you do? In this case the amount of your lead becomes the deciding factor. If you are way ahead, by three table-maximum bets or more, you should apologize to the blackjack goddess for any bad things you or anyone else may have ever said about her. You are in good shape. It may not be perfect, depending on how many hands remain, but you should still feel good. I would bet the minimum. Doing this makes them catch me. You may, however, be ahead by less than three table-maximum bets. In this case I fall back on the old "be aggressive" strategy. I would match the highest bet of my two competitors.

There is really nothing magic about the three table-maximum bets threshold I used in the previous example. I choose it only because I feel extremely uncomfortable and nervous when I am behind by that amount—and nervous players make mistakes.

There is another situation which doesn't neatly fit into a general strategy category. This situation occurs anytime you are forced to bet before your competitor. Remember, in tournament blackjack you are required to bet and play in order, beginning with the first-base player. Since first base moves with each hand, half the time you will be required to bet before your competitor. This poses a problem anytime you are in a position where you need to bet the same, more, or less than your competitor. However, all is not lost.

Remember the three personality types you will likely be playing against? If your competition is Wimpy Wanda, she is going to bet small. If you are ahead, then betting the amount she bet the last hand will likely protect your lead. If your competition is Aggressive Arnold, you can be assured that he will place a large bet come hell or high heels. If you are trying to catch Arnold, then placing a small bet will likely be the right move. Believe it or not, your biggest worry occurs when Erratic Ed is your rival. Ed may do anything, and have absolutely no reason for doing it. When you are up against Ed, be aggressive and hope that he just goes away. I should point out that in some tournaments there will be sloppy players who insist on betting out of order. *Never be too quick to place your bet;* you never know when your competition will place their bet out of order and give you an opportunity you might not have had otherwise.

Occasionally you will find that your competition is educated, though up until now this has been rare. You will, of course, recognize them: They make every effort to match your bet when they are ahead, and bet more or less than you when they are behind. When these plays start occurring you will know that you have a truly worthy opponent. If you find that you are playing against another good tournament player, simply stay with your game plan and hope that something gives. After all, there are other players in the game and anything can happen. Watch for opportunities carefully, and be sure to take advantage of them. These often occur when another player gets into a threatening position and your nemesis decides to match that player's bet.

Options, Naturals, and Pushes

You have learned that doubling down and splitting pairs are strong player options, and that you should always take advantage of them when the right combination of cards exist. No exceptions, right? Right. You have also learned that there are times when you would never double or split. No exceptions, right? Right. Well, welcome to the wild and wacky world of tournament blackjack.

Let's say you are ahead and have the opportunity to match your opponent's bet. The dealer turns up a 7 and deals you a 9 and a 2. A very good double-down situation. But should you do it? If you double, you are no longer matching your opponent's bet, and if you both lose the hand, he gains. Doubling might not be the best way to protect your lead. On the other hand, suppose you are the other player. You're behind and your opponent is matching your bet. In that case there is no doubt. If you have a double-down situation, take it. If you are in the latter hands of the game, you may want to double or split anything in an effort to catch up. The first time I saw a player double on a 16 against a dealer's 10, I thought he was completely crazy. But he wasn't—he was taking every chance he could to take over the lead. He had the attitude.

Blackjacks (a two-card "21" or "naturals" as they are sometimes called) can play a big role in tournament wins. If you are ahead by more than your opponent can bet, be sure to take into account the possibility of him drawing a blackjack before you get too smug. I once won a tournament round because I drew a blackjack on the last hand. They play a big role, and can completely change a game. Just remember: blackjacks happen. Try to build your lead to where a blackjack won't hurt you, or pray for one if you need it.

Earlier, we eliminated pushes from the outcome discussion, but they do need to be mentioned. In the latter hands of a round they are generally nothing but bad news. If you are trying to catch up, then a push just puts you one hand closer to losing. If you are ahead, a push can be as bad as a loss. They are similar to blackjacks, so assume that they will occur at the worst possible time and try to put yourself in a position where they won't hurt too much. If you are behind, start your aggressive catch-up earlier in case you push (tie) a hand. If you are ahead, say a few words to the push princess (daughter of the blackjack goddess). You never know when she might help.

Bluff to Bust

Let's consider this lousy scenario. It is the last hand of a round and you are $100 behind. You are in a position where you have to bet before your opponent, and he matches your $200 bet. You are in deep trouble. The only way you can win the round is to win your hand while your opponent loses his. To make things worse, the dealer gives you a 5 and a 4, and turns up a 10 for himself! Your chances of winning the hand are not good at all.

In the above situation, you have to assume that the dealer has a 20 for his hand, and that the only way you can win is to draw to 21. With the lousy hand you were dealt, you have only about a 6 percent chance of doing that. But I remember reading somewhere that a dealer will bust 25 percent of the time with a 10 showing. So if you can get your opponent to bust, you have increased your odds of winning from 6 percent to 25 percent. Desperate times call for desperate measures. You may want to try my "bluff to bust" strategy. It has worked for me twice: once at home while practicing tournament play against Steven, and once in real play. Your opponent has to have "the attitude" for this to work, so be sure to analyze him before trying it.

Here is what you do. Be careful not to let any players or observers see

your hand. Act like you have a pretty good hand and just can't decide
whether to stand or take a hit. Look at your money and your opponent's
money and say to no one in particular, "I've got to win this hand to win
the game." Reluctantly ask for a hit—and hope for a low card! If you
draw a low card, say a 3, then give your best "I can't believe it" look,
slide your cards under your chips, clap your hands, and say, "Yes! Yes!
Yes!"

Your opponent will see a very excited lady who has just drawn a 3.
What is he thinking? Well, if you have done a good job, he thinks that
you hit an 18 and drew to a 21. He will know that he has lost the
tournament unless he also makes 21. If his attitude takes over, then he is
very likely to bust. When this happens, you have greatly improved your
odds of winning. The dealer still has to bust for you to win, but
sometimes that will happen. If it does, don't expect your opponent to
congratulate you. Once he sees that you won with a 12, he is likely to be
something less than a good sport! Well, he shouldn't have let a woman
bluff him. Right?

Women in Tournaments

Contrary to regular blackjack, I don't think women have an advantage in
tournaments just because they are women; however, women seem to be
quite good at the game. In fact, on two occasions female players won
the National Finals Blackjack Tournament at the Riviera. A female
player also won the Celebrity Blackjack Challenge at the Rio.

These successes by female players should be an inspiration to the rest
of us. Learn my strategies, or Stanford Wong's, or develop your own,
and go for it! Enjoy yourself and good luck!

Chapter Overview

Blackjack tournaments are exciting; however, being successful in
tournament play requires a completely new set of strategies—and a
healthy amount of luck. Our more important tournament strategies are
listed below.

1. Develop "the attitude."
2. When ahead, use the "same" strategy.

3. When behind, use the "more or less" strategy.
4. When way behind, try the "long shot."
5. Be more aggressive than normal.
6. Analyze the other players.
7. If really desperate, try the "bluff to bust" strategy.
8. Talk to the blackjack goddess—you are going to need her.

12

"Okay, Steven, You Can Say Something!"

It was against my better judgment, I mean, to let Steven say something. We often sat at the kitchen table discussing the draft of one of my chapters and he always wanted me to add something regarding the history or the "why"—why it works, or why the statistics make this better than that, or...why, why, why. I wouldn't let him, because, well, it's boring. But he finally whined enough and I let him write a chapter all his own. I did make him change parts of it so you wouldn't need a dictionary on one side and a statistical book on the other to understand it. Actually, it's not bad. Please remember, though, all opinions are his and not necessarily those of the author—particularly those about slot players. Don't tell him, but now and then I still like to drop a coin in a slot machine.

—ANGIE

Casinos are fascinating. Few businesses could exist without supplying you a product or service at a reasonable cost. What do casinos provide? They take your money and offer you what? Adult recreation? Maybe, but I think they sell anticipation, hopes, dreams, and promises. After all, the casinos offer the possibility of turning one dollar into a million. People are lured by the promise that it *could* happen to them. Last year more than forty-five million Americans spent twenty billion dollars while visiting casinos.

Casino managers are very resourceful. Their job is to make money—your money. Experience has taught them the rate at which they can take your money without having you stomp off the premises with disgust, never to be seen again. In fact, if they provide the right atmosphere (glitter and glamour), and some free stuff (drinks and meals), and then tease you (with occasional wins or jackpots), they can take your money and still offer the anticipation, hopes, dreams, and promises necessary for you to return to fuel their huge money-gobbling machines—and their machines are immense. One Las Vegas casino had gambling revenue totaling $28 million the first two weeks after opening. That's two million dollars per day...at one casino! And there are hundreds of casinos across the country, all with huge appetites.

Casino Games

If you visit casinos, there are two terms that you should be familiar with: independent trials and dependent trials. Casino games are such consistent moneymakers (for the casino) because of the first term—independent trials. Roulette, slots, craps, and keno are examples of casino games that have set casino odds. Each event, whether it is a roll of the craps dice, a pull on a slot handle, or a spin of a roulette wheel, is unaffected by the previous roll, pull, or spin (or any other previous event). People continue to play them because they believe differently. I have repeatedly heard people say "This slot hasn't hit a jackpot all week, so it's due." Well, it makes no difference. If a slot machine hasn't paid in the last ten thousand pulls, that doesn't influence the outcome of the next one. Independent trials. I have seen people place large bets on red at a roulette table because "it hit black the last three times." It makes no difference. You guessed it—independent trials. People lose fortunes trying to beat these games using a "system." It won't happen. The truth is, if you play these games they will take you money. If you play them long enough they will take all your money.

Slot machines are the most intriguing of all casino games. Slots are somehow able to romance you. You will see people, both men and women, stalking the rows of machines in search of "the one" that's just waiting for them to sit down before belching its fortune into their laps. Some ladies believe that playing multiple machines is the secret to success, and they have developed a ritual that they use while playing four or five machines at once. They will dance from machine to machine, inserting coins and pushing buttons with considerable speed and grace. These ladies also maintain constant vigilance for other players who might be foolish enough to enter their domain, with hostile stares presenting a warning to anyone who approaches. These ladies remind me of a female mountain lion who is always eager to protect her home range: A fight to the death could develop if another lion trespasses on her territory.

Slot machines are placed side by side in multiple rows. When you are in their midst, you can hear the music of coins dropping from a machine into its payoff tray. This "music" sings the song of encouragement for other players to continue to seek their fortune. Angie even saw a television special discussing the casino's successful experimentation with perfumes that are being used at the slots to further the romance. The casinos will do anything to get people to lose their inhibitions and common sense.

Slot machines remind me of con artists. Con artists are successful because they romance, providing hope and promise in order to get their hands on valuable money—and then forever disappear into the sunset. Yet the same people who curse con artists will willingly sit down in front of a slot machine. They are romanced, and provided with hope and promise. The machine then takes their money and tucks it safely away. The players were conned by a machine! To make matters worse, the machine doesn't disappear into the sunset—it simply sits there flashing its lights, luring its next victim. It's absolutely amazing. Casinos make 70 percent of their profit from slot machines.

You might be getting the idea that I have a low opinion of casinos.

Not true. I really like casinos, but I do have a low opinion of their games—with one exception.

Blackjack

Blackjack. What an impressive game. It is the only casino game where the outcome of a hand is dependent on the cards played during the previous hands—*dependent* trials! This fact is what makes it the only casino game that can be beaten—and beaten badly. It is also what makes casino bosses hyper and paranoid—because they know it too.

The beginning of successful strategy blackjack actually started in the mid-1950s. Four scientist who loved to play blackjack and who were familiar with scientific procedures decided to try to reduce the casino advantage by developing a proper way to play every single hand. They started by identifying every possible two-card combination a player could get against every possible dealer up-card. Then they would play cards while considering all the player options (hitting, standing, splitting, or doubling) for every combination. Thousands and thousands of hands were played and the results were recorded and analyzed by hand. They had no computers, just clanking adding machines and Big Chief tablets. Their task took months, but their results produced a very accurate method of play (now known as the basic strategy), which virtually eliminated the casino advantage. The scientists (Baldwin, Cacty, Maisel, and McDermott) published their results in the *Journal of the American Statistical Association,* and received wide acclaim for their work. More importantly, in the early 1960s, the published paper caught the attention of Dr. Edward O. Thorp, a mathematics professor at the University of California.

Dr. Thorp began to formulate a hypothesis. Could the cards played during one hand influence the outcome of the next? Could this game of chance actually be a game of dependent trials? Dr. Thorp had access to stone-age computers that could slowly grind out results using reasonably sophisticated statistical programs. The results of his studies were astounding. He established, without doubt, that a deck rich in low cards was significantly in the casino's favor, and a deck rich in high cards was very much in the player's favor. Not only did he discover strong dependent trial traits, but also developed the first card-counting system that determined if the casino or the player had the advantage at any given time. He presented his conclusions at an annual meeting of the American Mathematical Society in Washington, D.C., and immediately drew national attention.

One thing led to another, and Dr. Thorp finally agreed to let two wealthy gentlemen finance a test of the system. It was conducted in Reno, Nevada, and Dr. Thorp turned their $10,000 investment into $21,000 in less than a week. During the process he was barred from several casinos. One thought his glasses were special and that he could actually see through the cards! He proved, however, that the system worked. Then he wrote *Beat the Dealer*, which quickly became a bestseller. Dr. Thorp was the first to prove that blackjack was a game of dependent trials. He was also the first card-counter to be kicked out of a casino. What a guy!

Well, when Dr. Thorp's book hit the streets the casinos went berserk. They imagined that their great money-gobbling machines would starve and die of bankruptcy. Some locked their doors, while others changed the rules so that no one could win, using *any* system. People quit playing blackjack because the horrible rules guaranteed quick losses, and the casinos started losing money. Eventually they were forced to go back to more liberal rules, and when they did, an amazing thing happened. Their profits skyrocketed. Dr. Thorp's book stirred a great interest in blackjack, but his system was very hard to learn and use, so few readers were willing to spend the time necessary to master it. Casino managers were elated, but remained extremely paranoid.

Extensive statistical work has been completed since Dr. Thorp did his study. The exact value of the cards has been calculated and count systems have been developed that are relatively easy to learn and use (in this context the value of a card means it contribution to either a casino or player advantage). Modern count systems use a simple plus or minus assignment of numbers to each card, based on its value to either the player or casino. Unfortunately, count methods are not perfect. Card-counting provides the player with two very important, but very different, opportunities. The first is the opportunity to bet more when the remaining cards favor the player. The second is the opportunity to play hands differently based on the relative density of low or high cards remaining in the deck or decks. Both of these opportunities significantly contribute to the player's advantage, but they create havoc to the statistical development of the "best" system.

The count system that provides strong statistical reliance for betting is different from the one that provides the best results for playing your hands. Since maintaining two separate counts for all the cards played is impossible, compromises have to be made. I use a level-two count system that provides an average 1.6 percent advantage over the casino. Overall, this is about as good as any man should expect.

Angie and I developed her strategy-play system after "backing into it." She uses a pretty good level-one count method, but the strategy play (her SIPS charts) was developed for our partners game, using decision indices based on my experience. She wasn't about to attempt to learn another set of decision charts when she started playing alone (that was an absolute), so some modifications were in order. I wasn't real comfortable with her decision numbers because we were adding compromises to compromises. I shouldn't have worried. The benefit she gains from being able to get by with a higher bet spread (just because she's a woman) more than makes up for any deficiencies in the strategy (because the more you can bet in favorable situations, the higher your percent advantage). Overall, whether she participates in our partners game or plays alone, she generates an approximate 1.8 percent advantage over the casino. That's better than my prized method! She uses 1.5 percent throughout her book, which is certainly accurate, although, in my opinion, a wee bit conservative.

What, Only 1.5 Percent?

At this point you may be quite unimpressed with a system that provides a meager 1.5 percent advantage over the casino. Seems awfully small, doesn't it? Let me put it in perspective for you.

Let's say an individual has $20,000 to invest and decides to put half of it into a good growth fund (stocks or whatever) that produces a solid 10 percent annual return. His fund investment would produce a $1,000 profit during that year (could be a little more if the dividends were calculated monthly and reinvested). Not a bad return. Now, let's suppose he decided to take the other $10,000 and go to the blackjack tables with a system that provides an expected 1.5 percent player advantage. His $10,000 stake would provide reasonable protection of an average bet size of $50 per hand. An average of sixty hands per hour are played at a blackjack table, and a system player can effectively play about six hours per day. The casinos use a term called "action per hour," which is simply the average bet size ($50 in this case) times the number of hands played each hour (an average of sixty). For this player, the action per hour is $3,000. Based on six hours of play per day, his investment into the game each day is $18,000 ($3,000 an hour × 6 hours = $18,000). A meager 1.5 percent advantage would generate an expected win of $270 per day ($18,000 × .015 = $270). If expenses averaged $70 per day, then $200 profit per day would be realized. Five days of play would generate the same return ($1,000) as the favorable fund investment generated in a year! Of course, more frequent play would generate more income. If he decided to play frequently and reinvested his winnings into his gambling stake, he would soon have adequate funds to significantly increase his bet size. He could be making more each day than his other investment was making in a year. All of this potential from a meager 1.5 percent advantage!

Well, If It's That Easy, Why Isn't Everybody Doing It?

I didn't say it was easy! But that is a legitimate question. In my opinion, all casino blackjack players fall into one of the following categories.

Those who don't believe or don't want to believe   These are strictly gamblers. Emotion and superstition totally drive their actions. Casinos cherish these people.

The wannabes   These players actually believe that blackjack can be beaten, but are only interested in a system that can be learned while on the airplane (destination Las Vegas). These people lose lotsa money.

Those who kinda learned a little   These players actually kinda studied, kinda learned to count, and kinda memorized a strategy playing chart. These players kinda get beat.

Those that learned good, but gave up   These individuals learned to play well enough to win, but immediately got caught in a negative swing. They got disgusted and quit. Lack of determination, coupled with a limited understanding of the game, led to these players' demise.

Those that learned good, but got kicked out This player is similar to the prior example, but instead of getting caught in a negative swing—he simply got caught. He played well enough to win, but was spotted by casino personnel as a card-counter and was politely asked to leave and not return—ever. This player then quit. He lacked determination, would not work on his emotions (getting kicked out is unnerving), and did not have a full understanding of "the game" (the *casino* game, between the skilled player and the suspicious casino boss).

Those with small-stakes disappointment This player did it all (almost). He learned to play blackjack, he respects the casino "game" with the pit bosses, and he wins, but his limited gambling stake dictates a small average bet, which translates into small returns. More often than not, he is unable to win enough to cover his trip expenses. He quits because the effort required to stay proficient is just not paying off. I have more sympathy for this player than any of the others who have failed. He is actually doing the right thing by playing with small stakes early in his endeavor and all he lacks is a longer-term view.

The successful player This player really did it all. He learned to play blackjack (it's not all that hard), learned to deal successfully with the casino "game" (common sense), and methodically built a playing stake adequate to provide substantial profit (discipline). He is a winner.

Chapter Overview

Okay, I'll sum it up. In my opinion there are three important (equally important) aspects of playing successful blackjack.

1. Mastering the Actual Game of Blackjack

This includes the actual mechanics of counting, betting, and playing your hand based on the count. This is not nearly as hard as most people make it out to be. You do have to study and practice, but not real hard and not forever.

2. Mastering the Casino "Game"

Knowing how to play will do you no good whatsoever if the casinos won't let you play. Learn how to deal with this. Learn how to play and win—without being caught.

3. The Gambling Stake

This can and should start small. Then it should grow as ability and desire for higher profits increases. It is an important aspect that many potentially good players neglect.

13

Casino Lingo

Learning the language is the essence of any endeavor.

—ANGIE AND STEVEN

Adding (your hand) The process of determining the sum of the cards dealt to you, Often difficult for the beginner, especially when Aces are included, but becomes second nature with practice.

Action A term used by casinos to describe the amount being bet by a player, usually expressed in action per hour; i.e., a player betting $5 per hand for one hour (assuming sixty hands are played per hour) would have a total action per hour of $300.

Advantage Term used to describe the odds a casino has over the player, or the player has over the casino; usually expressed as a percent. Casinos appear to have a 2 to 5 percent advantage over the average player, but players can develop a 1 to 2 percent advantage over the casino with skilled play.

Basic (Basic Strategy) A term used to describe a playing strategy in which the player plays each hand according to set guidelines. This type of play significantly reduces but does not quite eliminate the casino advantage.

Betting The process of placing a bet or wager. It must be an amount at least equal to the table minimum, and no more than the table maximum. Betting must be completed before the first card is dealt at the table. Touching your bet after the game has started is prohibited, or at least looked on with great suspicion.

Betting Circle   The spot on the table indicated by a circle, square, or symbol where the player is to place her bet.

Bet Spread   Describes the difference between the smallest and largest bet a player is making, and is often expressed as a ratio; i.e., a player who bets a minimum of $5 and a maximum of $25 has a bet spread of 1 to 5.

Blackjack   The game you are learning how to play; the only casino game that can be beaten in the long run with skillful play. Also called "21." Also the term used to describe a ten-value card and an Ace on the first two cards dealt to the player or dealer. Blackjacks normally pay 3 to 2 to the player (you would get $7.50 for a $5 bet).

Blackjack Goddess   This goddess roams every casino looking for players to assist. Occasionally she gets confused and cannot tell the difference between a player and a dealer (you will always recognize when this has occurred). Some players don't believe in the blackjack goddess, but they probably don't believe in Santa Claus, either.

Bosses   Refers to both floormen (or women) and pit bosses.

Burn Card   The top card of a newly shuffled deck, taken out of play by the dealer's placing it in the discard tray. Some casinos may burn one card for each deck in play; i.e., at a six-deck game, six cards may be burned.

Bust   Term used to describe a hand that exceeds a total of 21. Also called break. If the player busts it is proper to immediately turn the cards face up on the table. The dealer will then gather the cards and the bet.

Buy-in   A phrase used to describe the process of buying chips when a player first sits down at a table. No change is given at a blackjack table, so you cannot give the dealer $50 and ask for $30 in chips and $20 in cash back. (Well, I guess you can ask, but don't expect to get it!)

Cards (Card Values)   The cards are valued for the purposes of adding your hand, as follows: 2, 3, 4, 5, 6, 7, 8, 9 and 10 are as indicated, with Jacks, Queens, and Kings valued as 10, and Aces valued as 1 or 11 (at player's discretion).

Checks Play   A term used in the form of an announcement by the dealer to the floorman or pit boss when a player raises her bet significantly. The policies on this vary, but usually occur when a player raises her bet to five times the table minimum; i.e., if I bet $50 at a $10 minimum table I would expect the dealer to announce, "checks play."

Chips (Checks or Cheques)   Round tokens used in the place of real money when playing blackjack. Chips are usually labeled with the casino name and are in various colors which are usually standardized to indicate their value, silver or white, $1; red, $5; green, $25; black, $100, Five-dollar chips are called nickels, $25 chips are called quarters, and $100 chips are called bucks.

Comps (Complimentary)   A term used to describe free meals, drinks, rooms, shows, travel expenses, or anything. This is offered by the casinos to players based on a formula that considers hours played and average bet. (Sometimes you have to ask for a comp before it will be offered.)

Color Up   A process of exchanging lower-valued chips for those of higher value, i.e., exchanging five red chips for one green one. When you leave a table the dealer will often ask if he can "color up" your chips.

Counting   A term used to describe the process whereby a player keeps track of the cards as they are played to determine if the player or the casino has the advantage. Normally based on a plus or minus value assigned to the cards. Other count methods are sometimes used, such as 10-count, 5-count, Ace-count, and others. Counting is not illegal, but the casinos have the right to ask you to leave if they think you have an advantage over them.

Count   Term used to describe the relative advantage or disadvantage a player has at any point during a game; i.e., a plus count means that the player has the advantage, while a minus count indicates that the casino has the advantage. A $+5$ count is better than a $+1$, and a -5 is worse than a -1. Betting and playing usually varies, based on the count.

Count-Dependent Play   Describes a method of playing your hands (a variation of basic strategy) depending upon the density of high or low cards remaining to be played.

Cover   A term used to describe a playing tactic or style used by card-counters to hide their playing skill to more closely resemble the average player. Relaxing, having fun, and making careful bet spreads are examples. Sometimes called camouflage or act.

Crutch   A term used for various techniques some players utilize to assist them in maintaining the count. For example, stacking chips, positioning rings, feet, arms, hands, drinks, and so forth.

Cut   The process by which the deck or decks are split after each shuffle. A plastic card (cut card) is generally offered to one of the players, who then places it in the deck, and the dealer then moves the cards in front of the cut card to the back of the deck. Most casinos have a policy that a minimum number of cards be cut from the front or rear of the deck, usually no less than eight. The player can refuse the cut, and it is then passed on to another player, or if no other players are present, the dealer will generally cut.

Deal   The process of distributing the cards to the player; conducted by giving one card to each player, beginning on the dealer's left and proceeding clockwise to the last player on the dealer's right. After each player is given a card the dealer gets one, and the process is then repeated.

Dealer   The person who deals. This person is also responsible for all activities at that table, including buy-ins, settlements, administering house rules, and collecting tips.

Deck   A normal fifty-two-card deck (no jokers or promotional cards included). Casinos use from one to eight decks at blackjack games, with the odds in favor of the casino increasing with each deck added.

Defense (Defensive Play)   A term to describe plays that reduce the loss associated with a lousy hand, i.e., splitting a pair of 8s when the dealer has a 10 up.

Double-Down   An option offered to the player whereby she can double her bet by placing an amount equal to the first bet *beside* the first bet in the betting circle, and then receiving one, and *only* one, additional card. On many occasions this is a highly advantageous option for the player.

Double Exposure   Kind of a "show me yours and I'll show you mine" game, in which the dealer exposes both of her or his cards at the time of the deal. Rules for this game change to where, among other things, pushes are won by the dealer. This is definitely a casino-advantage game and should be avoided.

Even Money A term used to describe a player's request to receive even payment for her bet (not 3 to 2) when the player has a blackjack and the dealer has an Ace showing. The request must be made before the dealer checks his hole card. Should *not* be requested unless you are counting cards and know that it is advantageous. Taking this option when the count is high enough provides the same win expectation as the insurance bet.

Expectation Used to describe what a player expects to win or lose at a given percent advantage or disadvantage. The actual win or loss will seldom exactly meet the expectation. The likelihood of reaching the expectation increases with more hours of play (see *Swing*).

Eye-in-the-Sky Video cameras built into the ceiling above the blackjack tables; used to watch tables from a room somewhere in the casino. Used to settle disputes, watch for dealer compliance with house policies, to catch cheaters (dealers or players), and to detect card-counters.

Face Up (Face Down) Describes whether a card is showing its numerical value (face up) or showing the design pattern common to all the cards in the deck (face down). One of the dealer's initial two cards is dealt face up, with the other face down (often called the hole card); After a game has started, most hits are dealt face up, except those dealt to a double-down hand or to split Aces. In some games, all the players' cards are dealt face up, including those to double-downs or to split Aces. Face-up dealing is done to prevent damage to the cards as a result of handling and to prevent a player from intentionally marking the cards. In face-up games you are not supposed to touch your cards. Dealing face up provides no advantage to dealers because they must play by set rules.

First Base The player position to the dealer's far left. The player in this position is the first to be dealt to, and the first to play her hand.

Floorman (Woman) The individual who supervises the dealers and can often be seen watching the games from inside the pit. This individual works for the pit boss.

Hand Signals   Used by a player to indicate a request to hit or stand. The hit request is signaled by gently scratching the first two cards on the table, or in a face-up game by scratching the table with your fingers. The signal to stand is given by sliding the edge of the cards under your bet, or in a face-up game by waving your hand left to right, palm down, over your cards as though you were trying to see if any heat was coming off of them. When you push (tie), the dealer will pat the table with his hand. Hand signals are required as a matter of policy in most casinos because the eye-in-the-sky has no ears (at least we don't think so).

Hard Hand (Soft Hand)   Hard hands are those which do not contain an Ace, or hands which contain an Ace or Aces valued as 1 and the hand's total is 12 or more; i.e., an A,3,9 hand has a hard value of 13 $(1+3+9=13)$, while an A,7,10 hand has a hard value of 18 $(1+7+10=18)$. A soft hand contains an Ace which is valued as 11; i.e., the A,9 hand has a soft value of 20 $(11+9=20)$, while the A,A,7 has a soft value of 19 because only one of the Aces can count as 11 $(1+11+7=19)$. The A,7,10 hand *cannot* be soft because the player would have busted with a total of 28 $(11+7+10=28)$, so this one stays a hard hand with a total of 18.

Heat   Describes the action taken by a floorman or pit boss if they suspect a person is counting cards. Normally results in close scrutiny, instructions to the dealer to shuffle less than halfway through the deck, or instructions to shuffle every time that player raises her bet. Getting kicked out of the casino is the ultimate heat.

Hit   Used to describe the process of receiving another card to complete your hand. (Also describes what I do to Steven under the table when he looks at the cocktail waitress a little too long.)

Insurance   An option offered to players when the dealer has an Ace up. You take insurance by placing an amount equal to half your original bet in the insurance band, found just above the betting circle on most tables; insurance pays 2 to 1 if the dealer has a blackjack. When the dealer has a blackjack, you lose your original bet, but winning the insurance bet causes you to break even, hence the term *insurance*. If the dealer does not have a blackjack you lose your insurance bet and the game continues as if nothing had happened, with you playing your hand against the dealer's ace. Insurance has big odds in favor of the casino and should *never,* be taken—unless you are counting cards and know that the odds are in your favor!

Level (Counting Level)   A term used to describe the plus or minus value given to individual cards being counted; i.e., when none of the values exceed $+1$ or -1, then it is a level 1 count, if none of the values exceed $+3$ or -3, then it is a level 3 count.

Money Plays   An announcement by the dealer when a player chooses to bet cash instead of chips in the betting circle.

Natural   A term used by casinos to describe a blackjack; also called a snapper (I don't know why).

Parlay   A term used to describe a method of raising a player's bet from chips won on the previous hand; also called letting it ride.

Partners   A method of play in which two or more players at a table are helping each other. Steven and I use this method frequently to increase our advantage and to reduce the risk of being detected as card-counters.

Peeking   A term used to describe the process by which a dealer checks her or his hole card when they have an Ace or a 10 up; many casinos now use gadgets to handle this, and some do not allow dealers to check under 10s because of "tells." Also describes a method of cheating whereby the dealer peeks at the top card and then deals the first or second card, depending on which would be to his advantage.

Penetration   The depth into a deck a dealer deals before a shuffle. (The deeper the penetration the better we like it.)

Pit   The area behind the blackjack tables occupied by dealers, floormen, and pit bosses.

Pit Boss   The person who supervises the floorman. Will generally be seen roaming the pit or standing at a podium shuffling papers or entering data into a computer.

Push   Used to describe hands of equal totals between the player and the dealer. Pushes are not won by either side, except in some strange variations, such as Double Exposure.

Session   A predetermined amount of time to play at a casino; usually no more than one hour, but this is flexible.

Settlement   Used to describe the dealer's process of paying, or taking, the bets following the completion of a hand.

Shift   Describes a workday for dealers and bosses. A shift can be from midnight until 8 A.M., 8 A.M. until 4 P.M., or from 4 P.M. until midnight. Normally the entire pit crew, including dealers and bosses, will change between shifts.

Shoe   A boxlike device used to deal cards from; located at tables that use more than two decks.

Shuffle   The process of mixing the cards into random order. They are not always random, but will sometimes "bunch up," which allows card-counters to be successful.

SIPS (Significant Points)   Describes running-count totals which are significant for betting and playing your hands. Eliminates the need for corrections to true count. Not common casino lingo—yet.

Split (Splitting Pairs)   An option offered to players when the first two cards dealt are of equal value, whereby the two cards can be split into two hands and each hand played separately. Requires that the player place another bet equal to the first. The player is normally given the additional option of splitting again and placing another bet if another card is received with the value of the original pair (up to four splits are usually allowed). Aces are exceptions, and when split, you will generally be given only one card for each Ace. This option is valuable to the player.

Spreading Bets (as opposed to bet spread)   The option of betting on more than one betting circle. Can be done only if the adjoining circle is not occupied by another player. Most casinos require that you bet at least twice the table minimum on each hand if you spread your bets. You are generally not allowed to look at the second (or third) hand until you have completed the prior hand. You are, however, allowed to look at all your hands prior to playing them if the dealer has an Ace up (so you can decide if you want to insure them).

Stand (Stay)   What you do when you declare that your hand is good and you don't want any more cards. (See **Hand Signals**)

Stiff (Stiff Hand)   A term used to describe a hard total of 12 through 16 when the next card could bust the hand.

Strategy (System)   Used by players to gain an advantage over the casino. May refer to how a player plays her hand or how she bets, or both.

Surrender   An option offered at some casinos whereby a player may forfeit half of her bet to get out of the hand. A valuable option to the player. This is normally allowed only on the player's first two cards; it is generally not allowed before the dealer checks for a blackjack (late surrender). If you are allowed to surrender when the dealer has an Ace up but before checking for a blackjack, then it is called an early surrender, but this is seldom allowed (all references in this book are to late surrender).

Swing A term used to describe a decrease or increase in your gambling fund that is different from the expectation. This is statistically predictable, but a negative swing is disgusting, nevertheless.

Table (Blackjack Table) An oval-shaped table where blackjack is normally played. It usually has betting circles and chairs (stools) for seven players, although some have places for only five or six. It will contain an insurance band, rules that the dealer must follow, a shoe (if more than two decks are being used), a chip tray, a slot where currency is deposited, a card discard tray, and a small sign indicating minimum and maximum table bets. At some low-stakes casinos the tables will have two betting circles for each player.

Team Play A method of playing whereby several card-counters will spread out at blackjack tables in a casino and send signals to roaming players who will then place large bets at tables where there is a positive expectation of winning.

Tells A term used to describe the body language of a dealer after checking the hole card to determine if he or she has a blackjack. Includes dilation of pupils, standing back, leaning forward, and many others; used by skilled players to predict the value of a dealer's hand.

Third Base This player position is to the dealer's far right. The player in this position is the last to be dealt to and the last to play her hand. Other players will often hold the third-base player responsible for how the dealer's hands turn out.

Tipping (Toking) A common practice in which players tip the dealers for their service. This can be done by giving the dealer chips or by placing a tipping bet at the top of a betting circle before the beginning of a hand. If the player wins after placing a tipping bet, the dealer will pay the two bets (yours and theirs) separately, but if the player loses then both bets are lost to the casino (most dealers prefer the betting method of tips). Overtipping is very costly to the player and should be limited to situations when some advantage might be received, i.e., to entice deeper penetration before a shuffle.

Triple Action   A variation game in which the player has three hands and the dealer uses the same up-card for three hands. If the player busts on one hand then all hands are lost; definitely a casino-advantage game.

True Count   Describes the count after correcting for remaining decks or partial decks to be played (see *SIPS*).

Unit   A term used to describe a table-minimum bet; i.e., a player betting $5 at a $5 table is betting one unit; a player betting $25 at a $5 table is betting five units.

14

Before the End

Just some Women
    playing their game
They think we don't know how
    oh, what a shame!

Their chandeliers sparkle
    motivating our play
But we don't let the glitter
    get in our way.

Slowly, secretly,
    one small piece at a time
The chandeliers become ours
    to have and to shine.

              —ANGIE

Well, lucky ladies, you now know everything I know, and everything I think I know. Put it to good use and make them pay for their attitude toward us. I believe that most casinos have too many chandeliers anyway, and some of them would look good in your home. If you do your part, I promise to do mine.

Remember: Be careful. Don't let the glitter influence your play. We want the casinos to continue to believe we pose no threat, so take their chandeliers a little piece at a time. After all, *we do have an image to maintain!*

REFERENCES AND RECOMMENDED READING

One of the greatest gifts to give, or to receive, is
knowledge

—ANGIE

Books

Anderson, Ian. *Turning the Tables on Las Vegas*. New York: Random House, 1978.

Carlson, Bryce. *Blackjack for Blood*. Santa Monica, Calif.: Compustar Press, 1992.

Curtis, Anthony. *Bargain City*. Las Vegas: Huntington Press, 1993.

Dalton, Michael. *Blackjack: A Professional Reference*. Merritt Island, Fla: Spur of the Moment Publishing, 1993.

Griffin, Peter A. *The Theory of Blackjack*. Las Vegas: Huntington Press, 1988.

Humble, Lance, and Cooper, Carl. *The World's Greatest Blackjack Book*. New York: Doubleday, 1980.

Patterson, Jerry L. *Blackjack: A Winner's Handbook*. New York: Perigee Books, 1981.

Revere, Lawrence. *Playing Blackjack As a Business*. Secaucus, N.J.: Carol Publishing Group, 1980.

Rubin, Max. *Comp City*. Las Vegas: Huntington Press, 1994.

Thorp, Edward O. *Beat the Dealer*. New York: Random House, 1966.

Uston, Ken. *Million Dollar Blackjack*. Secaucus, N.J.: Carol Publishing Group, 1993.

Wong, Stanford. *Casino Tournament Strategy*. La Jolla, Calif.: Pi Yee Press, 1993.

————. *Professional Blackjack*. La Jolla, Calif.: Pi Yee Press, 1981.

Newsletters

Current Blackjack News (Stanford Wong) Pi Yee Press, 7910 Ivanhoe No. 34, La Jolla, California 92037.

Las Vegas Advisor (Anthony Curtis) Huntington Press, 3687 S. Procyon Avenue, Las Vegas, Nevada 89103.

Special Acknowledgement

Most of the inspirational quotes contained in this book were used with permission from *Bits & Pieces*. This excellent monthly publication is available from Economic Press, Inc., 12 Daniel Road, Fairfield, New Jersey 00704.

Sources for Supplies

Bud Jones Company, 3640 S. Valley View Blvd., Las Vegas, Nevada 89103; (702) 876-2782.

Gambler's General Store, 800 S. Main St., Las Vegas, Nevada 89101; (800) 322-CHIP, (702) 382-9903, or fax (702) 366-0329.

TEAR OUTS

Casino Record Form

Date _____ Time _____ Casino _____

No. of Decks _____ Table Min. _____ Buy-in Amt. _____

No. of Players at Table _____ Rules _____

Won/Lost $_____ Dealer: F ___ M ___ Dealer Speed _____

Penetration _____ Table Atmosphere _____

How were you treated by: Dealer _____ Floorman _____

Pit Boss _____ Players _____

Were you tired? _____ Were you drinking alcohol? _____

Were there distractions? _____

How did you feel? Confident _____ Unsure _____ Intimidated _____

Did you tip? ___ If so, how much: Total $_____

Other Comments: _____

_____

Most of the information you will be recording is pretty straightforward, but some is subjective. The following are some suggested responses you may want to use:

    Dealer speed: slow, medium, or fast
    Penetration: bad (less than half of the deck or decks)
                 average (over half, but less than three-fourths)
                 good (three-fourths or more)
    Table atmosphere: intense, fun, sober, loud
    Your treatment: bad, okay, good, indifferent

Basic Chart (One Through Four Decks)

Your Hand	Dealer's Up-card									
	2	3	4	5	6	7	8	9	X	A
8	H	H	H	H	D	H	H	H	H	H
9	D	D	D	D	D	H	H	H	H	H
10	D	D	D	D	D	D	D	D	H	H
11	D	D	D	D	D	D	D	D	D	D
12	H	H	S	S	S	H	H	H	H	H
13	S	S	S	S	S	H	H	H	H	H
14	S	S	S	S	S	H	H	H	H	H
15	S	S	S	S	S	H	H	H	H	H
16	S	S	S	S	S	H	H	H	H	H
A,2	H	H	D	D	D	H	H	H	H	H
A,3	H	H	D	D	D	H	H	H	H	H
A,4	H	H	D	D	D	H	H	H	H	H
A,5	H	H	D	D	D	H	H	H	H	H
A,6	D	D	D	D	D	H	H	H	H	H
A,7	S	D	D	D	D	S	S	H	H	H
A,8	S	S	S	S	D	S	S	S	S	S
A,9	S	S	S	S	S	S	S	S	S	S
A,A	Sp	Sp	Sp	Sp	Sp	Sp	Sp	Sp	Sp	Sp
2,2	H	Sp	Sp	Sp	Sp	Sp	H	H	H	H
3,3	H	H	Sp	Sp	Sp	Sp	H	H	H	H
6,6	Sp	Sp	Sp	Sp	Sp	H	H	H	H	H
7,7	Sp	Sp	Sp	Sp	Sp	Sp	H	H	S	H
8,8	Sp	Sp	Sp	Sp	Sp	Sp	Sp	Sp	Sp	Sp
9,9	Sp	Sp	Sp	Sp	Sp	S	Sp	Sp	S	S
X,X	S	S	S	S	S	S	S	S	S	S

Changes to the Basic Chart for Five Or More Decks

Hit an 8 against a 6
Hit a 9 against a 2
Hit an 11 against an Ace
Hit an A,2 against a 4
Hit an A,6 against a 2
Stand on an A,8 against a 6
Hit a 6,6 against a 2

Practice Chart

Your Hand	Dealer Up-card	Your Hand	Dealer Up-card	Your Hand	Dealer Up-card	Your Hand	Dealer Up-card	Your Hand	Dealer Up-card	Your Hand	Dealer Up-card	Your Hand	Dealer Up-card	Your Hand	Dealer Up-card	Your Hand	Dealer Up-card	Your Hand	Dealer Up-card	Your Hand	Dealer Up-card
6,8	4	9,7	X	6,9	9	X,4	2	6,8	7	X,8	2	8,9	5	8,5	6	9,7	3	6,X	6	3,7	6
A,6	7	7,5	X	5,4	5	6,5	8	2,5	2	X,5	9	9,7	A	X,4	4	8,9	8	5,6	A	4,6	3
2,5	4	3,5	7	4,X	A	3,9	5	2,3	9	3,X	X	9,5	5	A,A	9	6,8	2	5,4	6	2,4	X
4,4	4	3,X	8	5,4	2	7,4	7	6,6	9	6,7	3	X,9	6	5,4	7	2,5	5	2,6	8	5,X	3
4,8	7	4,6	9	2,7	A	4,8	2	7,7	6	X,6	8	5,4	3	2,9	9	7,8	9	2,5	3	8,5	4
5,9	8	X,9	X	5,5	2	9,6	7	4,4	A	5,9	4	9,6	6	9,8	5	7,7	A	8,9	2	8,9	7
4,3	8	A,4	A	X,2	3	7,7	5	3,9	9	X,A	3	6,9	X	5,6	9	A,9	7	3,3	2	7,5	5
A,7	5	5,5	7	5,6	X	A,6	6	7,7	8	X,4	X	9,9	4	8,4	2	6,9	A	X,X	4	4,3	9
7,4	2	A,6	4	3,3	7	9,4	8	4,7	A	6,X	3	9,9	A	9,5	4	A,2	5	2,4	6	X,X	8
A,X	6	9,9	3	7,6	4	A,A	7	8,5	8	8,4	A	A,7	3	2,X	8	9,X	7	5,5	9	8,9	X
4,A	5	8,A	A	3,5	X	3,3	3	6,A	5	2,6	9	4,8	X	8,3	3	7,A	4	7,6	7	7,2	9
A,A	3	7,2	4	4,X	6	A,5	9	9,A	X	9,4	3	6,5	4	4,6	8	3,A	3	5,8	9	6,3	A
5,X	2	3,3	5	7,2	8	7,X	8	X,6	A	2,9	3	3,A	6	A,X	8	8,7	2	3,8	4	5,2	7
3,7	8	9,A	8	6,5	3	5,8	5	5,7	6	7,A	9	7,2	X	3,6	2	8,3	5	X,3	6	2,9	8
3,8	A	4,8	3	A,9	4	9,X	5	7,8	7	3,7	7	5,A	8	2,5	3	6,6	2	9,6	4	A,3	7
8,6	9	A,A	8	6,7	X	8,8	3	2,3	4	4,A	7	7,2	8	5,A	2	2,2	3	6,3	5	2,8	6
2,4	8	3,7	X	7,5	A	6,X	2	7,X	4	5,9	7	3,A	8	5,8	3	8,2	2	X,8	4	X,5	6
A,A	7	5,3	9	4,3	X	5,8	3	4,A	4	9,7	7	8,X	9	2,2	8	8,X	3	2,8	5	8,9	6
4,3	7	X,X	9	8,6	A	9,A	3	8,7	5	X,4	5	8,2	7	5,9	6	6,8	8	2,2	A	9,6	3
4,4	5	4,8	6	8,X	9	8,3	2	A,4	3	3,7	5	A,7	7	9,9	8	3,3	8	6,6	A	7,7	2
6,X	5	4,3	6	5,A	7	8,8	8	9,4	X	3,7	3	8,A	2	9,6	8	3,A	5	3,7	7	5,5	8
7,X	X	4,2	3	5,3	4	8,5	7	9,7	8	3,3	A	6,2	3	6,X	4	9,4	6	A,8	9	4,6	X
8,X	3	2,9	2	4,9	4	9,4	7	8,2	9	2,A	A	4,2	2	5,5	5	4,6	6	6,A	9	X,X	A

Practice Chart continued

4,6	2	7,2	5	X,7	7	A,2	8	9,2	A	5,8	4	6,3	7	8,8	4	9,4	2	X,2	2	9,3	4
8,A	7	8,3	8	7,8	8	X,6	X	5,9	3	6,3	6	A,2	9	7,4	6	6,8	5	X,7	3	4,6	4
A,A	5	6,X	7	X,8	8	4,9	A	9,7	2	6,6	6	7,5	9	X,7	6	8,X	5	A,8	3	5,5	4
9,A	6	X,3	9	7,3	A	X,X	3	3,3	4	2,3	9	X,X	A	2,9	9	6,5	6	A,5	5	8,7	6
4,4	2	X,4	8	5,7	7	6,7	A	X,5	4	A,A	2	7,7	7	4,8	8	A,6	2	6,3	4	9,9	2
8,8	9	7,A	6	9,5	A	7,6	5	6,2	2	9,9	5	5,3	A	A,4	6	6,7	9	3,5	3	2,5	8
7,6	6	6,4	A	7,7	4	7,4	3	6,5	9	X,9	2	2,2	5	8,8	A	6,5	7	9,4	9	5,4	7
X,3	A	4,7	5	6,6	3	6,A	9	X,X	6	5,4	9	8,8	2	A,3	4	3,8	X	4,6	7	4,5	A
6,3	5	4,4	3	5,2	9	6,3	6	8,2	X	2,3	7	7,6	8	A,4	2	6,4	4	8,6	X	8,4	4
A,7	2	6,3	8	7,9	6	X,8	A	9,7	4	8,2	A	2,4	8	9,9	9	3,X	3	2,8	4	6,7	2
7,4	8	X,2	7	7,4	X	5,7	4	2,7	2	A,8	4	9,2	X	2,6	7	7,8	8	8,6	3	2,2	8
8,3	6	8,7	A	2,6	4	7,5	2	X,9	3	A,7	X	9,9	7	8,5	6	A,7	7	3,4	A	6,6	8
9,2	5	A,3	2	5,7	8	6,6	6	X,8	X	8,8	7	9,5	9	7,3	2	3,7	7	5,5	X	A,A	4
5,6	2	4,X	9	9,2	6	5,9	X	3,4	4	9,9	9	3,9	7	X,5	8	7,7	3	5,4	4	7,9	5
A,5	3	3,6	9	9,9	6	8,8	X	2,A	4	2,6	7	3,3	6	4,4	9	7,X	4	3,5	5	6,3	3
6,6	8	6,A	X	6,6	5	7,5	3	2,2	2	9,8	A	7,X	A	6,8	6	X,6	4	5,5	3	2,2	6
3,9	A	5,X	5	6,6	7	A,6	8	A,4	X	7,7	4	4,X	7	8,8	5	3,5	X	A,A	X	4,3	2
8,4	5	8,X	6	8,3	9	2,6	X	2,A	3	X,2	X	6,9	8	X,5	6	7,4	3	X,3	3	4,3	5
8,8	6	3,2	8	5,5	A	3,9	3	9,A	5	5,8	2	7,7	X	9,3	8	4,4	4	4,2	4	4,4	6
4,7	9	6,A	A	8,2	3	4,9	5	2,2	7	A,A	5	2,7	3	3,2	A	4,4	6	2,6	6	A,4	9
2,3	X	6,9	2	2,2	4	A,2	6	3,5	8	3,2	6	4,2	5	3,9	2	9,X	8	A,8	8	3,9	X
9,A	2	2,X	5	5,5	6	2,2	9	3,A	X	4,4	8	3,9	6	5,A	3	3,3	X	8,A	X	4,3	3
9,2	4	A,8	6	5,4	8	A,5	A	X,X	2	4,4	X	4,A	8	2,X	5	2,3	2	5,A	2	8,7	4
5,2	6	2,4	9	A,2	X	8,7	3	A,8	5	4,X	3	2,5	8	2,8	6	3,2	5	X,3	4	2,7	7
2,X	8	5,X	X	2,A	2	X,9	4	2,A	7	X,3	5	A,A	X	3,A	8	5,A	6	3,X	7	2,X	9
8,3	7	3,A	A	6,A	3	3,3	9	4,2	A	7,9	9	9,8	3	X,X	7	3,A	9	7,A	A	X,8	7
X,7	5	7,X	9	7,3	A	X,X	7	9,8	A	9,A	A	X,9	9	X,5	A	9,A	A	X,9	A	X,2	A

Count-Dependent Playing (8 Through 16)

Your Hand	Dealer's Up-card									
	2	3	4	5	6	7	8	9	X	A
8	H	H	H	+*D H	−H D	H	H	H	H	H
9	−H D	−H D	−*H D	−*H D	−*H D	+*D H	H	H	H	H
10	D	D	D	D	D	−*H D	−*H D	−H D	+*D H	+*D H
11	D	D	D	D	D	D	−*H D	−*H D	−*H D	−H D
12	+*S H	+S H	−H S	−*H S	−*H S	H	H	H	H	H
13	−*H S	−*H S	−*H S	−*H S	−*H S	H	H	H	H	H
14	−*H S	−*H S	−*H S	S	S	H	H	H	H	H
15	−*H S	−*H S	S	S	S	H	H	H	+*S H	H
16	S	S	S	S	S	H	H	+*S H	+S H	H

The asterisk symbol (*) signifies SIPS

Count-Dependent Playing (A,2 Through A,9)

Your Hand	Dealer's Up-card									
	2	3	4	5	6	7	8	9	X	A
A,2	H	H	−H / D	−H / D	−*H / D	H	H	H	H	H
A,3	H	+*D / H	−H / D	−*H / D	−*H / D	H	H	H	H	H
A,4	H	+*D / H	−H / D	−*H / D	D	H	H	H	H	H
A,5	H	+*D / H	−*H / D	−*H / D	D	H	H	H	H	H
A,6	−H / D	−*H / D	−*H / D	D	D	H	H	H	H	H
A,7	+D / S	−*S / D	−*S / D	D	D	S	S	H	H	+S / H
A,8	S	+*D / S	+*D / S	+*D / S	−S / D	S	S	S	S	S
A,9	S	S	S	+*D / S	+*D / S	S	S	S	S	S

The asterisk symbol (*) signifies SIPS

Count-Dependent Playing (Pairs)

Your Hand	\	\	\	\	Dealer's Up-card	\	\	\	\	\
	2	**3**	**4**	**5**	**6**	**7**	**8**	**9**	**X**	**A**
A,A	Sp	Sp	Sp	Sp	Sp	Sp	Sp	Sp	Sp	−*H Sp
2,2	H	−H Sp	−*H Sp	Sp	Sp	Sp	H	H	H	H
3,3	H	+*Sp H	−H Sp	−*H Sp	Sp	Sp	H	H		H
6,6	−H Sp	−*H Sp	−*H Sp	−*H Sp	Sp	H	H	H	H	H
7,7	Sp	Sp	Sp	Sp	Sp	Sp	H	H	−H S	H
8,8	Sp	Sp	Sp	Sp	Sp	Sp	Sp	Sp	+*S Sp	Sp
9,9	−*S Sp	−*S Sp	−*S Sp	−*S Sp	−*S Sp	S	Sp	Sp	S	S
X,X	S	S	S	+*Sp S	+*Sp S	S	S	S	S	S

The asterisk symbol (*) signifies SIPS

Count method

Card Value	2	3	4	5	6	7	8	9	X	A
Count Value	0	+1	+1	+1	+1	0	0	0	−1	0

SIPS Chart

Decks Remaining	SIPS
7	(+ or −) 35
6	(+ or −) 30
5	(+ or −) 25
4	(+ or −) 20
3	(+ or −) 15
2	(+ or −) 10
1-1/2	(+ or −) 8
1	(+ or −) 5
1/2	(+ or −) 3

Surrender

	Dealer's Up-card		
Your Hand	9	X	A
14	+ SIPS	+	+ SIPS
15	+	+	+
16*	+	+	+

*Split if it is an 8,8 against a 9.